CLAIMING HER MATES: BOOK TWO

DIA COLE

Claiming Her Mates: Book Two

Published by Black Diamond Press LLC.

Cover Art by Addendum Designs

Edited by Anne-Marie Rutella

ISBN: 978-1-946975-22-5

Once she saves his life, he'll have hell to pay...

Riding out the apocalypse with my sexy mates in a luxurious mountain lodge sounds like a dream. But for some asinine reason, Liam, Mason, and Gabriel have adopted a hands-off policy.

Even worse, my ex hasn't met up with us as promised. If sexual frustration doesn't kill me, my growing anxiety over the missing Alpha male might.

The only solution is to teach my mates a scorching lesson in satisfying my needs and launch a rescue mission. Nathan may have betrayed me and broken my heart, but I won't let him die. At least not until I've given him a piece of my mind...

For my miracles...

PROLOGUE

Nathan

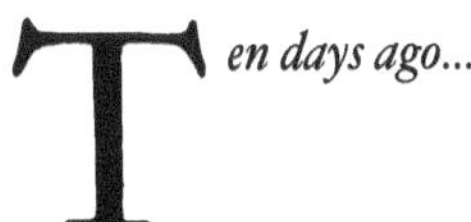

T*en days ago...*

A FURY OF SNOWFLAKES LASHED MY WINDSHIELD AND buried familiar landmarks in an icy grave. *Damn the fates.* Not even the enhanced vision gifted to me and others of the Lykos species allowed me to see through the oncoming blizzard.

I tightened my grip around the steering wheel and faced the unfortunate truth that it was too dangerous to continue up the mountain. Cursing under my breath, I pulled the Range Rover onto the shoulder of the two-lane mountain road. Squinting, I could barely make out the snow-laden sign for the Sunridge ski resort. *I'll have to stop there for the night.*

Damnation. For months I'd been forced to keep my distance from my female and now she was so close.

Vana.

A vision of her long dark hair and curvaceous body flashed in my mind. I'd missed the stunning beauty with every fiber of my being. Trying to go through my duties as the Winterhaven Ambassador while pretending I wasn't missing the other half of my soul had been pure hell. Having to sleep in our bed without her smooth warm skin pressed against me. Having to eat meals without her banter over the dining room table. Having to walk through the estate without hearing the click of her stiletto heels on the marble floors. But now, finally, I'd get to see her. Touch her. Beg her to forgive me for betraying her trust.

She didn't know I'd cast her aside in order to save her life. She didn't know that horrible night I'd planned on proposing to her, not ending our relationship. But all my plans had gone up in smoke the second I'd discovered that Tasha Digoski, the psychopathic Alpha of Winterhaven, had broken into my home and murdered every human she'd found inside.

Thank the fates Tasha hadn't realized what Vana really meant to me and thank the fates the she-bitch hadn't been able to locate my daughter. No doubt, Tasha would have tortured and murdered Mira too.

Shuddering, I glanced into the rearview mirror.

A pair of sleepy eyes, the same golden color as mine, stared back at me.

"Are we there, Daddy?"

"Not yet, sunshine."

"I want to see Vana," Mira said through a long yawn.

"And you will," I promised. The little girl had taken the loss of Vana almost as hard as I had. And no wonder, Vana was the closest thing she'd ever had to a mother.

"Okay," Mira said with absolute trust in my word. She rested her small head against the window, her eyelids heavy.

"Sleep, sunshine. I'll wake you up when we get there."

She stiffened at my request. "I'm not sleeping."

I let out a heavy sigh. Although young, Mira was already a headstrong Alpha female who took orders about as well as I did. "Just rest your eyes then," I said in a gentle voice.

Mira had barely slept the entire drive. Unfortunately, traffic delays had turned what was supposed to have been a several hour trip into an overnighter. Reports on the radio indicated there'd been multiple crashes, but I suspected the bumper-to-bumper traffic was compounded by the influx of humans fleeing north.

They, like me, were trying to outrun the pandemonium in town. They, like me, were trying to outrun the apocalypse.

For weeks I'd been entirely focused on my carefully orchestrated plans to take down Tasha. So much so that I'd ignored the reports of cannibalistic humans and the discovery of the Z-virus. Like a fool, I'd bought the CDC's explanations that the new virus was similar to rabies and it only appeared as if people rose from the dead. Who cared about some hysterical humans when the entire future of my faction depended on the strategic alliances I was making with Tasha's enemies?

However, the moment Tasha's Enforcers, Gabriel and Liam, showed up on my doorstep to evacuate me, I knew the medical community had been hiding the truth. People were turning into zombies and human civilization was on the brink of collapse.

Now all that mattered was getting the two females I loved to safety. I'd rescued Mira from her new nanny's home in the nick of time and I prayed to the fates that Tasha's Enforcers, who I'd compelled to save Vana, had done their jobs. Needing to be sure they also weren't stuck in this storm, I pulled out my cell phone and dialed Gabriel's number.

He picked up on the first ring.

I didn't mince words. "Is Havana safe at Sanctuary?"

"Yes," he replied, sounding as if he was chewing glass. Tasha's Head Enforcer was used to barking orders, not taking them. Being compelled to do my bidding clearly wasn't sitting well.

His attitude couldn't dampen my relief at hearing Vana was safe. "Good."

Picking up on our conversation, Mira began kicking the back of my seat. "Vana! Vana!"

I twisted around and held a finger to my lips. "Shh. Quiet, Mira. You'll see her soon."

Mira pouted adorably.

"You didn't tell me Havana was a latent," Gabriel said in an accusatory tone.

Surprised, I nearly dropped my phone. *How does Gabriel know Vana's a latent?* So far my best friend Ty and I were the only ones who knew that Vana was a Lykos who hadn't yet transitioned. We'd done everything in our power to shield her from the other Lykos, especially Tasha. *Vana can't have started her transition yet.* Just a few weeks ago, Ty had assured me Vana wasn't showing any signs. He'd been watching over her for me until Tasha ordered him back to Winterhaven.

"Does Havana know what she is?" Gabriel continued.

Fuck no. I'd deliberately kept the truth from Vana. The less she knew, the safer she'd be from Tasha. I knew I couldn't keep it a secret forever, but somehow sharing the truth with Gabriel before telling Vana herself seemed like even more of a betrayal. *What choice do I have?* Gabriel had obviously already put the pieces together. I didn't trust the Head Enforcer as far as I could throw him, but I could always wipe his memory.

Rubbing the stubble on my chin, I let out a heavy sigh. "No. She knows nothing. When I first interviewed her for the nanny position, I sensed there was some Lykos blood in her—it's why I hired her in fact—but I assumed she was an Atavus." As a human born with trace amounts of Lykos blood in her, she was resistant to Mira's attempts at compulsion. That meant, unlike Mira's former nannies, Vana didn't cater to my daughter's every whim.

But Vana hadn't been a mere Atavus like her mother. I cleared my throat and continued. "My visceral attraction to her should've been a clue she was so much more. It wasn't until I dug into her background that I discovered she was a latent. Apparently, her mother had a one-night stand with a colonel before becoming pregnant with Havana." When Ty had revealed the intel he'd gathered about Vana's origins, I'd nearly had a stroke.

Gabriel went silent for a few moments. "I'm guessing not just any colonel."

No, not just any colonel. "I suspect he was one of the original test subjects from the Lykos project." All evidence indicated that Vana's father was likely Zacharias, one of the oldest, strongest, and most powerful of our species. Although the military had reputedly destroyed most of their initial test subjects, a few like Tasha had escaped, and a few, like Zacharias had been retained as soldiers.

Gabriel cursed. "You know we're required to report any suspected Lykos to Tasha and—"

Absolutely not! "Tasha can't know about Havana. I'd planned to take her and Mira somewhere far from her territory." First, we had to meet up with a rival faction leader at Sanctuary.

Gabriel snorted. "Well, obviously that didn't pan out. Havana's close to her transition so you'd best not take too much time getting back here. I can barely keep Liam and Mason away from her as it is."

What? Blood roared in my ears. I bared my teeth, my inner wolf clawing to the surface. "She's mine! I will eviscerate any male that touches her. Understand?"

"Why are you yelling, Daddy?" Mira cried from the back seat.

I covered the phone and said, "It's okay, sunshine." I took a deep breath and let it out. The idea that Vana was transitioning and going into her first heat brought out my territorial Alpha nature. I'd worked hard over the years to temper my savage instincts, but when it came to my female, all bets were off.

Damnation. Her transition couldn't come at a worse time. It meant a definite change of plans. I'd have to take Vana somewhere private for at least twenty-four hours. A Lykos female in heat needed to mate constantly and I wouldn't tolerate any other males around. My mouth dried as I imagined what the next few days would have in store for the two of us. *Vana will forgive me. She'll claim me. Then she and I will mate until our bodies give out.*

"Understood," Gabriel said, dragging me back to our conversation.

"Good." Gabriel's respect eased some of my tension. The need to see Vana burned inside me, but outside the wind was picking up. I turned on the windshield wipers and peered ahead. I could barely see more than a few feet. *Fuck.* I slowly pulled the Rover back onto the ice-covered road and updated Gabriel on our change of plans. "The storm is closing in and I won't risk the drive up the mountain with Mira. Sunridge is here on our left. I'm pulling into the resort. Mira and I will stay here for the night. Expect us first thing in the morning."

"Yes, sir."

I ended the call and drove into the ski resort's parking lot. Not surprising this close to Christmas, it was only half-full. *Good.* The fewer the humans, the less likely anyone with the Z-virus was inside. Stopping here was a calculated risk, but if this storm was as bad as they were predicting, it'd be too dangerous to sit it out in the car. I needed my daughter warm and dry and if that meant taking out a zombie or two, so be it.

"Is Vana here?" Mira asked, her eyes dancing with excitement.

"No, but we're going to stop here for a little while."

"I want to see Vana. No stopping." Mira crossed her arms over her chest and gave me a mutinous look.

Curse the fates, if she's this much of a handful at four, what will she be like as a teenager? Shaking my head, I tried another tactic. "I'll bet they have pancakes. Do you want pancakes for breakfast?"

She shook her head. "Do they have pizza?"

Pizza for breakfast? If Vana were here, that'd be a no go. *Ah hell, why not?* "Yes, they definitely have pizza. Let's go get some."

Mira perked up. "Okay!"

I checked my suit pockets, looking for my wallet. *Hell, tell me that in my hurry to pack all our things, I didn't leave that behind.* Thankfully, I found the wallet inside my suit breast pocket along with Vana's engagement ring. I brushed my fingers against the four-carat diamond and made myself a promise. *This time tomorrow, Vana will be wearing this.*

Grinning, I opened the car door, stepped out, and helped Mira out of her booster seat. Then with her little hand clasped in mine, we walked up the snow-covered walkway to the hotel and went inside.

Odd. Why isn't there anyone at the front desk?

I

HAVANA

A shot of adrenaline spiked my blood as two giant wolves tried to bring me down. The silvery-white snow crunched like broken glass under my paws.

Gabriel, the dark brown wolf, stayed on my left flank, while Liam, the massive russet-colored wolf, pressed in on my right.

"Stop, Havana!" Gabriel telepathically ordered. *"We're almost at the wall."*

As if his words conjured it up, the eighteen-foot stone wall that protected Sanctuary, the forty-acre property where we were riding out the apocalypse, appeared in the distance.

Almost there. I increased my pace.

"Enough!" Gabriel shouted into my mind. *"You know the rules. Stop!"*

"It's not safe," Liam added.

I was sick of safe. I was sick of pacing the floors of the luxurious winter lodge pretending the world wasn't imploding. But most of all, I was sick of them treating me like a fragile doll that could shatter at any moment. It'd been a week since either of them had touched me. I gnashed my teeth in frustration.

I might have tolerated the lack of intimacy better had it not been Christmas Eve, the anniversary of my mother's death.

Remembering my mom brought back bittersweet memories. She'd been MIA most of my childhood, but she'd been the only family I'd had. Scratch that, I had a new family. One I'd created by claiming the sexiest three guys I'd ever met.

One of those guys was back at the lodge trying to find a cure for the Z-virus using his medical expertise. The other two were hot on my heels.

Seeming to realize I wasn't stopping, Gabriel and Liam both rushed forward and tried to tackle me to the ground. But I was too fast. In a burst of speed, I darted past them and bounded over the wall in a single physics-defying leap.

Crunch.

I landed in the middle of a snowdrift, the soft impact not slowing me in the slightest. With a toss of my muzzle, I shook off the feathery flakes and continued loping down the road. In just minutes, I came to a small run-down cabin.

Funny how a little more than a week ago, I'd risked death itself to escape that place. Of course I'd been dying of the zombie-plague so braving a snowstorm to seek help from Mason, Liam, and Gabriel seemed the lesser of two evils.

Thankfully, Mason had cured me and sent me into my first werewolf transformation. That triggered my first heat cycle, which resulted in me claiming him, Gabriel, and Liam as my own.

My breath came faster as I remembered all the ways my sexy mates and me had mated. It'd been incredible. The scorching memory of our foursome in the shower kept me from sleeping most nights. I physically ached for more. But my mates apparently didn't feel the same. I'd done everything

I could to stir their interest including become a nudist around the lodge, and still they kept me at arm's length.

Never in my life had I been this needy. It was as if my Lykos transformation had flipped me into some kind of sexual hyperdrive. The sexual frustration along with the mounting anxiety each day that my ex, Nathan, and his young daughter didn't arrive was driving me insane.

My heart ached as I thought of little Mira, who I used to nanny. She and her father should have been at Sanctuary ten days ago, but there had been no sign of them and, without working cell towers, we had no way of contacting them. For all I knew they hadn't even made it out of Saguaro Valley, one of the epicenters of the outbreak.

They could've been attacked. My stomach churned at the thought of Mira being hurt or worse. Her father, on the other hand, could become zombie food for all I cared. Three months ago, the rat bastard had ripped my heart out and stomped all over it when he'd kissed his supposed dead wife in front of me. To add insult to injury, Nathan proceeded to tell me our relationship had meant nothing to him right before he slammed his front door in my face.

All those times he'd told me he loved me. *Lies.* All those plans we'd made. *More lies.* Nathan's betrayal had shattered my naïve belief in love and happily-ever-afters. The only good to come out of that experience was I'd learned how to claw myself out of the depths of depression, and Nathan had, in a roundabout way, introduced me to my mates.

Although Gabriel had tried to convince me that Nathan might have ended our relationship to save me from Tasha, the vicious Alpha of Winterhaven, I didn't entirely buy it. Nathan had been too cold. Too cruel that night. And that kiss he'd given Tasha had looked plenty real to me.

I growled as Tasha's model-perfect face came to mind. *Fuck her.* It didn't help that my mates were fixated on her too.

They all seemed to live in fear of her arrival. Sanctuary was her vacation home and my mates were supposed to be her loyal subjects. Apparently, the statuesque blonde would murder us all on sight for taking what was hers.

I snorted. *Let her try.* The psychotic bitch had forced Gabriel to kill his own family and tortured him for years afterward. I looked forward to avenging his pain.

The sound of panting breaths made my heart race. *They're gaining on me. Can't let them catch me...yet.*

With a single bound, I landed on the rickety wooden steps of the cabin and immediately took my human form. The first few times I'd reshaped my body had been disorienting. However, after practice, shape-shifting had become second nature, just like the ability to shield my thoughts from my mates. Thrilled they'd have no idea what I had in store for them, I yanked the front door open.

The sharp, sweet scent of the peppermint oil Liam had used to drive off the former furry occupants of the cabin beckoned me inside. The cozy interior, with the large windows overlooking the frozen river out back, was almost the same as I'd remembered. Of course, the fire in the woodstove had gone out. But it wasn't as if my bare skin even registered the cold. One of the many perks of being a Lykos.

Sitting across from the rocking chair and leather recliner was the bed where I hoped the next stage of my plan would land me.

My favorite boots, black dress, and long charcoal wool jacket lay on the soft white cashmere area rug next to an IV stand. Mason must've taken off my wet clothes to warm me the night he found me freezing outside. I wrinkled my nose at the sight of the coagulated bag of blood still attached to the pole. *Ugh. Tasha's blood.* Although a transfusion of her blood had healed and transformed me into a rare and powerful Alpha female, it made me sick to think some part of that monstrous woman was running through my veins.

Deciding that the IV stand was a mood killer, I walked in, grabbed it, and wheeled it to the far corner of the cabin. Then I hid it behind the curtain Mason had hung around a bedpan. Thank God, I'd been able to upgrade my accommodations before I'd been forced to use the makeshift bathroom. I'd never take running water and electricity for granted again.

The sound of stomping feet on the wood steps outside was my only warning before the cabin door flew open and a scowling, naked, dark-haired man stormed inside.

Gabriel's eyes glinted with anger. "Havana, what's the meaning of this?" His ragged breathing brought my attention to the smooth bronze muscles of his chest.

Unable to help myself, my gaze dipped lower to his six-pack abs, and then even lower to the delicious package hanging between his legs. I bit back my moan. I couldn't wait to lick, suck, and bite every delicious inch of his powerful body. Playing dumb, I batted my eyelashes. "Are you upset about something?"

He ran a hand through his collar-length hair. "Fuck yeah, I'm upset. You know you need to stay behind the wall."

He looks so sexy when he's agitated. "Then it sounds like you need to punish me for breaking the rules." I knocked several pillows aside and crawled onto the bed. "Do you want to spank me?" I twisted around to present him with my naked bottom. Although as an exotic dancer I'd played at being a BDSM queen on stage, I'd discovered that I loved being dominated in bed.

No one dominated better than Gabriel. *Except Nathan*, a wicked voice inside my head whispered. I bitch-slapped that unwelcome commentary and focused on the dark-haired male.

Gabriel clenched his jaw. "Don't tempt me."

But that's exactly what I planned on doing. I gave Gabriel a coy look through my long dark hair. "If you don't correct me now, I might have to run away again and again…"

"Havana." His rumbling warning would've made any sane woman back down.

But mounting sexual frustration made me a bit crazy. "You should spank me."

He growled. His growing lust pulsed through our bond.

He wants me. Then why won't he give us what we both crave?

When he didn't move a muscle. I chewed on my lower lip. "Well, if you aren't man enough to give me the punishment I deserve then maybe—" I broke off when he crossed the distance between us in a blur of motion.

"You forget, I'm not a man at all," he growled, grabbing my hips.

Yes! "Take me," I pleaded, spreading my thighs. Rough. Gentle. Fast. Slow. I didn't care as long as he quenched this burning ache inside me. I rocked back feeling the scorching heat of his erection against my core.

He inhaled sharply and took a step back. "Princess, I can't."

"Why the hell not?" We'd already overcome his initial reluctance to mate with me because he'd thought of me as Nathan's female. *What's his hang-up now?*

"We don't want to hurt the babe," a deep, rumbling voice said from the doorway.

I looked around Gabriel's shoulder to see a gorgeous seven-foot-tall, auburn-haired, bearded male. "What baby?"

Liam strode in and shut the cabin door behind him. "The babe you're carrying."

Gabriel nodded. "It's important you take it easy right now. As much as I—" he looked over at Liam "—as much as we want to be with you, we don't want to jeopardize the pregnancy." He looked down at his bare wrist as if checking an imaginary watch. "We should get back to the lodge. Mason will have lunch ready by now. A female in your condition needs to eat regularly. Lykos pregnancies aren't like human pregnancies. The gestation takes less than half the time and is very demanding on the mothers."

I shook my head in disbelief. *They can't be serious?* I flipped over on my back and stared at the two of them. "I'm not pregnant. I have an IUD."

Gabriel's eyes widened. "You do?"

"Hell yeah, I do." I'd had the procedure done when Nathan and I first got together. All my life I'd wanted children, but I'd wanted them after I was married. I'd promised myself early in life that I'd never end up in my mother's shoes —partnerless and raising an unplanned child.

My stomach tightened as I thought of my mom again. Even though she and I had a complicated relationship, I missed her.

Liam strode over the wood floor and came to stand next to Gabriel. "What's an IUD?"

"I think it's a form of birth control," Gabriel answered slowly.

I sighed. Explaining contraception to werewolves was one of many conversations I never thought I'd have. "It's a device implanted inside my body that prevents me from getting pregnant."

"But you went into heat?" Liam said, looking confused.

I shrugged. "That wouldn't matter. I can't get pregnant until the IUD is removed." I'm sure when the time came, Mason would be more than happy to do the honors.

"But...but... Don't you want babes?" Liam asked, his gaze searching my face.

"Very much," I answered honestly. But I wanted it to be a planned event. My mom never let me forget I was a not so appreciated parting gift from a one-night stand. "Just not right now." Bringing a baby into the apocalypse wouldn't be the smartest idea even if the child would have some amazing daddies to look after him or her.

"So you're not pregnant," Liam said, his green eyes darkening.

"She's not pregnant," Gabriel echoed, reaching down to caress my breast.

"Not even a little." I moaned and arched into his hand. My nipple instantly hardened into a tight nub. "So are you two going to punish me for breaking the rules?"

"Hell, yes we are." Gabriel pinched my sensitive peak with enough pressure to take my breath away.

"You've been a very naughty female." Liam pinched my other nipple.

"Oh!" I gasped brokenly at the pleasure-pain sensation. My heart pounded with anticipation as I swept my gaze over the gorgeous naked males in front of me. It'd been so long and I needed this. I needed them.

✴ 2 ✴

HAVANA

Pushing Liam's hand away, Gabriel grabbed hold of my ankles and dragged me to the edge of the bed. He pushed my legs apart and brushed his thumb lightly over my sex.

I moaned and bucked against his touch.

"Look how hungry she is for us, Liam. She's already dripping wet." Gabriel slid two fingers inside me.

I whimpered at the erotic invasion. It felt so good.

Liam licked his lips and watched Gabriel's fingers thrusting in and out of my damp flesh. "She likes that?"

"She likes it very much," I panted. I rocked up off the chocolate-colored comforter, chasing Gabriel's fingers.

Gabriel clamped his free hand on my hip, locking me in place. "None of that. You take what I give you—nothing more. Understand?" He pulled his fingers out, reached up, and pinched my nipple.

"Yes," I hissed, my eyes rolling back in my head. "Please." The agonizing throb between my legs had me shifting restlessly.

Gabriel looked over at his friend. "Watch and learn,

brother. Our Alpha doesn't like it slow. Does she?" He slid three fingers in, and increased his tempo.

I cried out my approval. I loved the raw ferocity of Gabriel's lovemaking. He didn't do slow and sensuous like Mason. There was also never any sweet hesitancy to his touch like Liam. Gabriel fucked hard and raw. And right now that was exactly what I needed.

A savage hunger gripped me as I checked out the heavy muscles rippling under his dark bronze skin. *He's so goddamn hot.* I dropped my gaze to the heavy erection swinging between his thighs. I couldn't wait to feel his cock hammering deep inside me. And Liam's. I couldn't help but do a double take at Liam's massive erection. I grew wetter just thinking about fitting all of him inside me.

"Look at me, not Liam," Gabriel ordered.

A shiver went through me. I loved when Gabriel was bossy like this. *Nathan used to*—I crushed that thought before it could grow wings. Nathan was my past. Gabriel, Liam, and Mason were my present and future. I raised my gaze to meet Gabriel's.

"Good girl." His dark eyes blazed with wicked passion. "Do you want me to fuck you?"

"Yes." *So damn much.*

Gabriel pressed the head of his cock right where I needed it. "You want this inside you?" He dragged his hot, rigid flesh over my seam.

"Oh, God. Yes," I cried, rocking my hips forward.

"Then as part of your punishment, I won't fuck you." He pulled his hand and cock away.

"What? That's not fair." I tried to sit up.

"I say what's fair." Gabriel pushed me down. "Don't move unless I give you permission." He clamped his fingers around my clit.

Pleasure sizzled through my nerve endings. I arched off the mattress.

"Liam, how else should we punish this naughty female?" Gabriel gave my clit another pinch.

Liam's gaze lit up and he grinned at Gabriel.

Gabriel nodded in response to some silent telepathic conversation they were having. "Good idea." Then Gabriel climbed onto the bed. Before I could process what was happening, Gabriel pushed me into a seated position, with my legs hanging off the bed, and situated himself behind me.

I could feel his hard-as-steel cock against my ass. *Is he going to take me from behind?* "What's going on?"

"That's for us to know and you to find out." He reached around and clamped my nipples with his fingers.

I writhed in pleasure.

Liam got down on his knees in front of me. Despite his imposing size, he looked almost bashful. "I've always wanted to do this." He dipped his head down and kissed my knee. The whiskers of his beard brushed against the soft skin of my inner thigh.

I giggled.

Liam snapped his head up, looking confused.

I immediately bit my lip. *Poor guy.* He thought I was laughing at him.

"She's ticklish," Gabriel said to Liam. "But she won't laugh anymore, will she?" He twisted my nipples hard enough that I saw stars.

"No, I promise," I moaned.

"Keep going, brother," Gabriel ordered.

Liam blew a hot breath over my aching flesh. "Does this feel good?"

"Yes," I gasped, my entire body trembling.

"And this?" He pushed his face between my legs and licked.

The hot lash of his tongue on my sensitive flesh was so good it almost bordered on painful. "Oh, yes!"

Liam gave me a big smile. "You taste so sweet. I could do this forever."

"Make her beg for release." Gabriel tweaked my nipples again. "You're not allowed to orgasm until I say so, princess. Understand?"

"Y-yes," I gasped, wondering how the hell I was going to hold myself back.

Liam dove in, licking and sucking me senseless. Although he devoured my pussy with more enthusiasm than finesse, it was goddamn perfect.

My head fell back against Gabriel's chest as I gave myself over to the hot, wet friction of his mouth and tongue. Pleasure coiled tight inside me. I dug my nails into the side of Gabriel's thighs and held on to him for dear life.

"Here's another tip, brother." Gabriel reached down and spread my lips. "See that nub, that's her clit. Suck on it. "

Liam immediately drew my clit into his mouth eliciting a strangled moan from my lips.

Sizzling arcs of electricity pulsed through me. "I can't take much more!" My thighs trembled as I fought to hold back my orgasm.

"Oh, you'll take it," Gabriel growled into my ear. Then he looked down at Liam. "Fuck her with your tongue."

Liam spread my thighs wider and thrust his tongue deep inside me.

"Oh!" Erotic pleasure overwhelmed my senses. Gritting my teeth I tried to fight the mounting tension in my body.

Gabriel reached between us and pinched my clit.

It was too much. Liam's mouth. Gabriel's fingers. Blinding pleasure consumed me. I came hard, shaking between the two men like a rag doll.

When I'd finally stopped quivering from the aftershocks,

Gabriel made a tsking sound. "You didn't take your punishment, princess. Now we'll have to punish you some more."

I licked my lips, my breath going choppier. *I can't wait.*

Liam rocked back on his knees and looked up at me with dazzling green eyes. "Did you like that?"

Gabriel frowned at him. "Of course she liked it. Didn't you hear her screams?"

I leaned over and kissed Liam tasting my own musky flavor on his lips. "It was amazing."

My gentle giant beamed up at me. Once again I marveled that this sinfully handsome man had been a virgin until a week ago. There were so many naughty things I wanted to show him. I couldn't wait to—

"Stand up," Gabriel ordered, slapping my ass.

Blinking in surprise, I stumbled to my feet.

Liam reached out his hand to steady me.

My thighs shook as I stood at the edge of the bed.

Both Liam and I looked to Gabriel, waiting for him to command us.

Despite me being the Alpha, Gabriel loved to call the shots in the bedroom. Since I found it sexy as hell, I let him. "What did you have in mind?"

The dark-haired male moved to the edge of the bed and motioned down to his erection. "Take me in your mouth."

I leaned over, breathing in Gabriel's smoke and leather scent. Then I dipped my head and gave his cock a lick. The salty taste of him made my tongue tingle.

He let out a hiss of breath.

I grinned in feminine satisfaction. *I'll blow his mind.* Wrapping one hand around his throbbing shaft, I started to kneel.

"No, spread your legs," he said, wrapping his fist around my hair. "Liam is going to take you from behind." He looked over at Liam. "Get behind her."

Okaaay. This is new. I turned to look at Liam.

The big guy's eyes blazed with desire. Rising up slightly from his kneeling position, his giant cock brushed against my ass. The smooth head was already wet with precum.

Anal sex with Liam and no lube? Anxiety made my heart pound. I braced my arms around Gabriel's legs and tensed. I didn't think I was going to enjoy this.

Gabriel chuckled, reading my mind. "Relax, princess." He looked over at Liam. "Fix your aim."

Liam shifted underneath me. His steely hardness pressed against my core.

Much better. Biting my lip, I sank down on him. My breath caught as his massive cock filled me to the brim.

"Is that okay?" Liam asked, holding himself still.

I closed my eyes savoring the sensation. "Oh, yes." I swiveled my hips, loving the way he filled me so completely.

Gabriel tugged on my hair, drawing my attention back to him. "Make me come, princess."

"Oh, I will." Smiling, I took him in my mouth and pleasured him with my lips, tongue, and hand. Lucky for him, my best friend Syd had instructed me in the fine art of giving blow jobs. The trick was in varying the rhythm and, of course, deep throating was always a crowd favorite. Soon I was wringing moan after moan from Gabriel's lips.

"You're too good at this," Gabriel panted, thrusting against my lips.

"She is," Liam said, giving me a slow pump. "I can't wait for a repeat." He telepathically sent me the memory of his first blow job during our foursome in the shower. His excitement pulsed through our bond, making my core spasm.

"Come on, brother. Fuck her like you mean it," Gabriel chided, his fingers tightening in my hair.

"Like this?" Liam pounded into me deep and fast.

"Ah!" I moaned, feeling the drumbeat of another orgasm

building. I sucked harder on Gabriel as Liam moved faster underneath me.

"Fuck!" Gabriel's entire body stiffened. Then he cried my name and exploded into my mouth.

Once I swallowed every drop of Gabriel's cum, I pushed away and reared back on Liam's cock. The muscles in my thighs shook and burned with the effort of keeping myself poised over him.

Liam gripped my hips to keep me in place. Then still inside me, he turned us away from the bed and pushed me down on all fours.

I was barely aware of the rough wood floor digging into my palms and knees. In this position, he was seated so deep inside me it felt as if we were one. I squeezed my inner muscles urging him to move. "Fuck me, Liam. Fuck me, hard."

Liam made a low sound, something between a growl and a snarl. Then he slammed into me, over and over with such force it drove us across the floor.

It was good. *So good.* I lowered my head, lifted my ass, and rotated my hips to meet his thrusts. The heat in my belly coiled tighter and tighter.

Liam's cock swelled inside me. "I'm going to come!"

"Have some fucking self-control, brother. Pinch her clit," Gabriel called out.

The moment Liam clamped his fingers around my bud, a blast of heat shot through me. I came so violently a scream tore from my throat.

Liam let out an earsplitting roar. His cock jerked and he emptied his hot seed into me.

Completely wrecked, I nearly collapsed on the floor when Liam slid out of my body.

Liam caught me, drew me into his lap, and whispered in my ear, "Thank you, beautiful."

"No, thank you, big guy," I panted.

"I didn't give either of you permission to come," Gabriel shouted from the bed.

Liam rolled his eyes. "Fuck off, brothe—"

The cabin door swung open and hit the wall with a crack.

A strange woman in snow gear rushed into the cabin and aimed her shotgun directly at us.

❧　3　☙

GABRIEL

hreat! *"Protect Havana!"* I mentally shouted at Liam.

The large male pushed our female down and positioned his body over hers. He looked up at the gun pointed at his head and snarled. *"Get the weapon, Gabe!"*

I bounded off the bed, flew over Liam and Havana, and tackled the unfamiliar human. The weapon clattered to the floor.

Liam quickly grabbed the gun.

"I'm sorry. I'm sorry!" The human shrieked through a black face mask. "I thought someone was being hurt."

Not trusting the stranger for a second, I frisked her. When I didn't find any additional weapons, I tore off her goggles and balaclava. She looked to be in her late teens or very early twenties. Glaring into her bright hazel eyes, I said, "You will never pull a weapon on us again."

The heavy dose of compulsion made the female clutch the sides of her head. Tendrils of curly blond hair escaped her wool hat. "I won't," she said in a dazed voice.

"Tell us who you are," I demanded, keeping one hand firmly wrapped around her throat.

"I-I'm Tina. I'm a ski instructor at the Sunridge ski resort."

"Are you here alone?"

She shook her head. "N-no. I have kids with me."

Kids?

"Let me up," Havana shouted at Liam. When he didn't move, she shoved the several hundred pound giant over.

The reminder of her newfound strength brought my adrenaline down a few notches. Our Alpha was stronger than we gave her credit for. Case in point, she'd led us—two of the deadliest Enforcers in the Southwest—on a merry chase this morning. Still, it was our job to keep her protected. Havana was not only our ruler, but she was also our mate. I didn't like that this puny human female could catch us off guard. *We need to be more vigilant.*

"*Yes, we do,*" Liam said, reading my mind. "*I don't want this human anywhere near Havana.*"

That made two of us.

Unfortunately, Havana didn't feel the same. "Let her go."

"But—"

"Now, Gabriel." Havana's voice rang with power. There was no resisting the order.

With one last scowl, I released Tina's throat and rolled off her. Giving the human a warning growl, I took a protective position at Havana's side. The second Tina made another threatening move, I'd tear her throat out.

"Here, let me help you up." Havana offered Tina her hand.

Tina blinked at her and then at Liam, who stood on Havana's other side.

Havana rolled her eyes. "Don't mind them. They can be a bit overprotective of me."

The human ran her gaze over our bodies and flushed. "I didn't mean to interrupt..." She cleared her throat and looked away.

Havana blinked, seeming to realize we were all naked. "Oh. Uh. This is awkward. Liam, can you get me my dress? It's over there at the foot of the bed."

Liam handed me the shotgun and then retrieved the black dress Havana had been wearing when we first picked her up.

As she pulled the garment over her head she said, "Guys, cover up."

Liam dutifully grabbed a throw pillow from the bed and held it over his crotch.

I didn't move. Tina could be a spy for Tasha. I'd never known the Alpha of Winterhaven to use humans for anything other than target practice, but there was a first for everything.

"Gabriel," Havana said in a warning voice. "*Humans are uncomfortable with public nudity.*"

What the fuck do I care? "*We aren't in public. This human barged in on us. I don't trust her.*"

"*Please. For me,*" Havana pleaded.

Shit. When Havana looked at me like that, I could deny her nothing. "*Fine.*"

"*Here.*" Liam threw me Havana's jacket.

I caught it and belted the gray wool coat around my waist. "Better?" I said out loud.

Havana gave me a smile that under any other circumstances would've had me hauling her back to the bed, spreading her thighs and—

"You said you have kids with you?" Havana asked, jarring me from my fantasy.

The blonde nodded and got to her feet. "Yes, I made them wait across the road. We heard screaming, and I thought someone was being attacked. I-I'm sorry to bust in," she stammered, her blush deepening.

"They must be freezing out there. Have them come in," Havana said as Liam helped zip up the back of her dress.

I snorted. It was nearly as cold in here as it was outside. *"This isn't a good idea."*

"They're children," she said giving me a reproving look.

"I'll get the stove going," Liam offered.

Havana beamed at him. "Great idea."

I flipped him off. *"Way to make me look like the bad guy. We need to be protecting her."*

"I don't think she needs as much protecting as you think," Liam retorted, walking over to the woodstove.

"That's where you're wrong." It wasn't just the walking dead and strange humans we needed to watch for. *"Don't forget that at any moment Tasha could send a contingent of Enforcers to Sanctuary."* Or even worse, she could decide to pay a personal visit.

Liam's smirk faded at the mention of our former ruler and a sliver of fear flashed in his gaze. "Tasha's hands will be full for a while."

True. Once she'd become aware of the Z-virus outbreak, she'd recalled every member of our faction back to Winterhaven. But the chaos there would subside eventually, and her attention would shift. *"Eventually she'll come."* Tasha always came after her enemies. And that's what Liam, Mason, and I had become the moment we'd pledged ourselves to a new Alpha female. My gut tightened. Tasha was the strongest and deadliest female Lykos in existence. *There will be no escaping her wrath.*

Liam paled. *"Then we should go. Let's take Havana as far from Tasha's territory as we can."*

"We don't know what we'd face out there." Based on what we'd seen as we rushed Havana out of Saguaro Valley, we'd likely find nothing but carnage and devastation. The reanimated would've claimed most of the human population by now and though Liam and I were strong fighters, even we couldn't keep Havana safe from legions of zombies.

Then there was the fact that the lodge at Sanctuary was

equipped with everything we'd need to survive the apocalypse: large walls to keep out the reanimated, solar power, well water, and enough food and medicine to last for years. I groaned at the impossible decision we faced. *Death if we run. Death if we stay.* Honestly, I almost hoped that Nathan would get here despite the inevitable shitstorm of rage he'd direct at us for mating his female. The Alpha male said he had a plan to get Mira and Havana to safety. *I need to know what that plan was.*

Havana spoke softly to the human, "We have water and snacks here." She motioned at the water cooler and a crate over by the table.

Tina gazed up at me.

I bared my teeth and growled.

Tina backed away. "That's okay. We should keep going. We're heading to a place up the road."

"There's nothing up there but Sanctuary," I said, studying her through narrowed eyes.

"Oh, is that the name of the gated estate?" Tina said, looking flustered.

"Yes, we're staying there," Havana interjected. "But you're welcome to join us."

"No, she's not," I said, quickly. Over my dead body were a bunch of strange humans coming to the lodge.

Havana gave me a sharp look. *"Show some compassion, Gabriel."*

"Compassion gets people killed."

The human looked over at me and paled. "I-I hoped if I got the kids inside the walls there, they'd be safe from the zombies."

Interesting. The human has had run-ins with the reanimated. She could give us valuable intel. "How bad are things in town?" Sunridge, the town, was barely half a mile south of the ski resort.

"I don't know. I'm guessing bad." She swallowed hard.

Liam looked up from throwing a log in the stove. He looked ridiculous trying to start a fire with one hand while trying to keep the pillow strategically placed with the other. "What about the ski resort?"

Good question. During my last conversation with Nathan, he'd said he and Mira were staying the night there.

"I'm pretty sure everyone there is dead. Well, the dead that stumbles around trying to eat you." The blonde's eyes watered.

Did that mean Nathan and his daughter were dead? The idea filled me with a mixture of emotions. Remorse that yet another young Alpha female had perished. Relief that the one male who could seriously threaten my relationship with Havana was no more. Frustration that I'd never know the plan he had to get Havana to safety.

"How did you survive?" Havana asked in a gentle voice.

Tina wiped her eyes with the back of her gloves. "I had my class up on the lifts when another instructor radioed that all hell was breaking loose at the base lodge. He said we needed to stay away. I brought the kids to the Midway Café to wait for further instructions. Several skiers at the café went crazy and started attacking people. I tried to protect the kids, but..." She gulped in a deep breath, clearly still in shock.

"Tina, are you okay?" a young male voice asked from the doorway.

The human whipped her head around. "Isaac, I told you and Lily to wait for me."

"But we were worried," a younger female voice said.

Havana started for the door, but I beat her to it.

Gripping the shotgun tightly, I stared down at two small human faces.

The dark-skinned boy, no more than ten, wore a red wool

hat over his curly brown hair and clutched a thick tree branch in his gloved hand.

The girl wore a pink snowsuit and looked around the age of seven. Her long hair was as inky black as Havana's. The contrast between her bone-white skin and bright blue eyes reminded me of the porcelain dolls my mother had collected before Tasha forced me to kill her.

Fear wafted off the children as they stared up at me.

Havana pushed me out of the doorway with strength only an Alpha female could possess. "Come inside." She beckoned them to enter and then peered around them. "Are there more out there?"

The boy shook his head. "The others are dead."

Havana looked at Tina.

She rushed over to the kids and put her arms around them. "I had five in my class. The others...the others..." She started tearing up again.

The boy and girl stiffened. For the first time, I noticed the blood spatter across their jackets.

Obviously these kids had gone through some deep shit. Despite my better judgment, I could feel my resistance to helping them crumble.

Tina coughed and wiped her eyes. "We were able to hole up in the back kitchen of the café for over a week. But the zombies started breaking through the door. We managed to escape this morning. Instead of going down the mountain, I brought Isaac and Lily up here."

"And how lucky you did. We can protect you now." Havana gave Tina a warm smile.

Tina blinked, still looking wary. "Weren't you guys freezing in here without any heat?"

"We were keeping ourselves warm," Havana answered with an embarrassed smile.

"Right." Tina blushed again. "How did you get here? I mean... I didn't see a vehicle outside?"

"W-we, uh, walked," Havana stammered.

Fuck. The last thing we needed were some humans asking too many questions. I glared into the eyes of Tina and the kids. "You will not question anything strange, understand?"

Their three heads bobbed up and down obediently.

Havana gave me an annoyed look. *"Stop using compulsion on them."*

"Then make them leave."

She ignored me.

"How about some cocoa, kids?" Without waiting for a response, she padded over to the crate began rummaging through it. "Aha!" She held up a package of hot chocolate. "Do we have any mugs, Liam?"

The red-haired male nodded. "There should be some in the crate." He closed the door to the woodstove that was starting to give off heat. "Here's the kettle." Keeping one hand gripped on his pillow, he raised up a silver teakettle.

"Gabriel, can you help?" Havana asked, as she took Tina and the kids over to the wooden table and bench.

"Ah hell." I snatched the kettle from Liam's hands and trudged outside to empty it. The clouds were darkening as if in warning. We needed to get back behind the walls of Sanctuary without delay and we needed to leave these damn humans behind. Given how stubborn Havana was, I knew that wouldn't happen. With a sigh of resignation, I marched inside and filled the kettle with water from the water cooler. Then I handed it off to Liam. *"This is a shitty idea."*

Liam set the kettle on the stove and looked at Havana who was busy preparing snacks for the humans. *"Tasha would've killed all three humans on sight."*

"No. She would've hunted the females for sport and then kept the boy for...fun," I corrected.

"You're right." His eyes darkened with blood-filled memories. *"I much prefer Havana's way."*

"Even if it gets us all killed?"

"I don't fear death, do you?" Liam turned his gaze to mine.

"No," I answered honestly. I deserved death for the things I'd done as an Enforcer. But Havana didn't. *"I fear for Havana."*

We both turned to look at the beautiful female that had claimed our bodies and souls.

The instinctive, overpowering need to protect her rushed through me. *"We can't let anything harm her."*

Liam's expression tightened. *"We won't."*

As we watched Havana feed the humans, my chest tightened. *We can try to protect her from outside threats, but can we save her from herself?*

❦   4   ❦

HAVANA

After sending Liam back to Sanctuary to get his SUV, I had him transport Tina and the kids to the lodge.

Gabriel and I shifted into our wolf forms and followed the vehicle.

The entire way Gabriel lectured me. *"You're making a mistake. We know nothing about these humans."*

"I know enough." Tina and the kids were traumatized, and they needed help—help that we were able to give. My heart ached for what they'd gone through and for the children who hadn't survived.

Gabriel let out a heavy sigh that sounded more like a wolf wheeze. *"Then confine them to the lower level and have Mason check them out to ensure they aren't infected."*

Crap. I didn't even think about them being infected. Even though we were immune to the Z-virus, the idea we could have zombie children running around the lodge was enough to turn my stomach. *"We'll do that. But, assuming they check out, you need to be nicer to them."*

The brown wolf flashed me his long sharp canines. *"When am I not nice?"*

I snorted. I was quickly learning Gabriel had more bark than bite, at least with me.

As the SUV in front of us stopped at the front gate, Gabriel and I veered to the left. When we were a safe distance away, we bounded over the wall and headed up the long driveway to an enormous two-story lodge.

The luxurious ten-bedroom home still made my jaw drop. It had everything including fireplaces in every room, a huge kitchen, full-size library, three living rooms, a movie theater, and even a ballroom right out of Cinderella.

Liam actually apologized for the fact that the lap pool wasn't finished, but he assured me the Jacuzzi and sauna were in working order. Ha! As if that weren't enough, there was also an underground level almost as large as the main lodge. Although I wasn't a fan of traveling down to the bunker, I had to admit I was impressed with its row of lavish bedrooms, a kitchen, dining hall, infirmary, fully equipped game room, workout room, and storage rooms filled floor-to-ceiling with food, water, and other supplies. If not for the threat of the bloodthirsty owner showing up, Sanctuary would be freaking perfect.

"Mason?" I called out telepathically. I was still getting a feel for the psychic bond I shared with my mates. We couldn't communicate from long distances, but the more we "spoke" the easier it became to establish mental connections.

"I'm here, love," came Mason's sexy voice. I loved his British accent almost as much as I loved the naughty things he did with his talented mouth.

Before I could speak, Gabriel barged into our discussion. *"Did Liam brief you on the humans?"*

"Yes. I've prepped the infirmary and taken the liberty of bringing some lunch down to the lower level for them."

"Thank you," I said, my tone filled with affection. Although

I tried to hide it, my sweet, sexy doctor had cornered a large piece of real estate in my heart.

"Did I hear someone mention lunch?" Liam asked, pulling the SUV through the front gates.

Inwardly laughing at the big guy's fixation on food, I bounded to the top of the stone steps where Mason stood waiting for us.

The gorgeous blond doctor looked good enough to eat in khakis and a sea-blue polo that matched the stunning color of his eyes. He greeted me by holding out a buttery soft lavender wraparound dress. As always, he anticipated my needs better than I did.

In a flash, I took human form and belted the ankle-length gown around me. Standing on tiptoe, I brushed my lips against his. "Thank you, hon."

"What no clothes for me?" Gabriel asked, his tone dripping with sarcasm.

Mason ignored the brown wolf, his gaze focused only on me. "I missed you." He wrapped his tanned arms around me and dragged me into his broad chest. Although the doctor lacked the hulking size of Liam and Gabriel, he was plenty tall and muscular for a human. Much like me, he'd grown up ignorant of his Lykos nature. As a result, he and I bonded over our human way of thinking, something that irritated the heck out of Liam and Gabriel.

Mason's soothing rain scent washed over me as I melted into him. "We were only gone a few hours," I teased.

"That was a few hours too long." He inhaled deeply and drew back. "You had sex." He leveled an accusatory look at Gabriel.

"Lay off, Mason. She's not pregnant," Gabriel said, taking his human form faster than I could blink.

Mason frowned. "How could you know that? It's barely been a week—"

I interrupted the doctor. "I can't get pregnant, hon."

His blond brows rose. "What do you mean?"

"I have an IUD. There's no possibility of a baby."

"Oh." He frowned. "So all this time we've stayed away—"

"For no good reason," I finished for him. "We should make up for lost time." I leaned over and nibbled his earlobe.

He flashed me a wicked grin. "That's the best idea I've heard all week."

Liam pulled the SUV in front of the steps and jumped out. He'd thrown on boots, jeans, and a flannel shirt that clung to his thick biceps for dear life.

I hummed my approval as I waved Gabriel into the house. "You get some clothes on."

The dark-haired man looked like he would argue with me, but the sound of the kids squealing had him grimacing and stalking into the lodge.

Although I loved how he and Liam walked around naked most of the time, we would have to enforce a dress policy if we had guests staying with us. *Human guests.* For the first time a sliver of apprehension ran through me. *How are we going to keep our werewolf natures from them?*

Reading my mind, Mason reached over and grabbed my hand. *"We'll think of something."*

Liam caught my eye as he ushered Tina and the kids up the steps. *"Gabe already compelled them not to question anything strange."*

Tina's hazel eyes widened as she saw me by the door. She looked in the direction of the cabin and then back at me. "How did you—" She trailed off as her eyes glazed over. Her confused expression was replaced by a robotic-looking smile. "Nice to see you again."

Crap. I was so not a fan of mind control. *God only knows what kind of damage it does to people's heads.*

Mason reached in front of me and offered his hand. "You

must be the lovely Tina I've been hearing so much about. I'm Mason James."

Despite my anxiousness, a smile tugged at my lips. I found it endearing as hell that all three of my mates had taken my surname to show they belonged to me.

Still looking slightly dazed, Tina took his hand.

"Can you show them downstairs and check them for infection?" Gabriel's warning had gotten into my head.

"Of course."

While Mason brought our guests down to the infirmary, I ran upstairs for a quick shower and then went looking for Liam and Gabriel. I found my mates in the gymnasium-sized library.

Gabriel stood next to Liam wearing only a pair of jeans slung low around his hips. I really couldn't object at his loose interpretation of getting dressed when it put all his bronze muscles on display. I licked my lips in anticipation of a repeat of our hot session in the cabin.

Unfortunately, the men didn't look to be in the mood. Their expressions were tense as they hunched over a large antique-looking desk. They didn't speak, but based on the scowls they exchanged it was clear they were having a telepathic argument.

I let out a sigh. "What is it, guys?"

They jerked their heads up and gave me a guilty look.

"Nothing," Liam said much too quickly.

I walked over and peered between their muscular arms. There was a map of the area spread out over the desk. "What are you doing?"

Gabriel stepped to the side allowing me a better look at the map. "We're doing a threat assessment."

"Right," I said, acting as if I knew what that was.

Gabriel placed his finger down on the black star in the middle of the map. "Population estimates put the town of

Sunridge at eight hundred give or take. Worst-case, there are probably another couple hundred at the ski resort. If what the human says is true—"

I sucked in a breath. "Then there are potentially a thousand zombies down there right now."

Gabriel nodded. "Give or take."

My stomach swam with unease as I mentally calculated the distance between Sunridge and Sanctuary. It was close. Too close. *What's to stop the dead from coming for us?*

Reading my mind, Liam reached out and rubbed my arm. "Don't worry, Havana. The snow will keep them off the mountain."

"For now," Gabriel added, a grim look on his face. "When it melts the reanimated will go looking for food."

Translation, go looking for us. I swallowed hard. Based on the map, it looked like Sanctuary was the only residence in a forty-mile radius of the town. "They'll come here, won't they?"

Gabriel gave a curt nod. "They could surround the wall and trap us here."

I gasped.

Liam gave Gabriel a hard look. "We aren't even sure if the dead can climb the mountain."

"But we can't assume they can't. No one knows what these things are capable of," Gabriel replied.

A chill ran down my spine as I remembered my encounter with a group of zombies back at the club. Despite considerable damage to their bodies, they'd kept coming for me. Something told me that a mountain wouldn't get in their way.

Gabriel let out a deep breath. "Although not ideal, having a thousand reanimated at the wall may not be such a bad thing."

Has he lost his damn mind? "How do you figure?"

"They'll keep the Beast away," Liam said, a slow smile breaking out on his face.

Gabriel nodded as the men shared a relieved look.

I looked between them in confusion. "The Beast?"

"Tasha," Liam clarified. The flash of fear in his eyes when he said her name took me by surprise. My protective giant wasn't afraid of anything. *Right?*

How can they possibly prefer a horde of zombies to a single Lykos female? "What is it about Tasha that has you all so worked up?" I got the fact that she was an Alpha with the ability to compel Lykos less powerful that herself. But I'd been able to undo her compulsion on Gabriel, which made me think she would not be able to control my mind.

"Tasha's an Original," Gabriel answered. At my blank look, he continued, "Remember when I said the military genetically engineered our species?"

I nodded, thinking back to our conversation at the cabin a week ago.

"Well, Tasha was among the first Lykos the military created nearly a hundred years ago."

"A hundred years ago?" *No way.* "I've seen her and she doesn't look a day over twenty-five."

"The Originals don't age like we do. The military designed them to be stronger, faster, and more powerful than anything on earth."

"And more psychotic," Liam added.

Gabriel gave him a quelling look. "Because of their mental instability and their allegiance to their Alpha females over their human commanders, the military terminated most of them. However, a handful, including Tasha escaped."

How lucky for us, I thought bitterly. "Well, even if she's super strong and fast, we four can take her."

Gabriel let out a hollow laugh. "If only that were the case. The Originals can take hybrid form—"

"Become indestructible," Liam interrupted.

Gabriel growled. "I'm talking here."

"Sorry, go on." Liam waved his hand.

Gabriel turned back to me. "In her hybrid form she can regenerate any injury. I once saw her take an entire machine gun drum of ammunition to the chest and not even blink."

"I remember that," Liam said, chuckling. "That assassin screamed like a babe when she tore the weapon from his hands and then ripped out his spinal column one vertebra at a time. Didn't she try to feed the pieces to him too?"

Gabriel grunted.

"What?" My stomach churned. *Just how insane is this woman?*

Gabriel held my gaze. "Assassins from other factions have been trying to kill Tasha for decades. I've seen her survive being set on fire, blown up, and almost completely decapitated. Frankly, I'm not even sure she can be killed."

"Great." Just my luck that my arch nemesis would be immortal. I wet my suddenly dry lips. "So what do we do?" *How do you defeat something that can't die?*

Gabriel met my gaze with his steady dark eyes. "Let's start by seeing for ourselves what's going on at Sunridge and the ski resort."

"You're talking about us going down there?" I'd barely survived that club encounter and there had only been three zombies. My throat tightened at the thought of going up against a thousand of those things.

"Not us," Gabriel corrected. "Liam and me."

I shook my head already rejecting the idea. "No." I would never risk my mates like that. "It's too dangerous. Besides with all the snow, the road is likely impassable."

"We don't need roads." Gabriel's eyes gleamed. "There's a chopper stored in the hangar on the north end of the property."

"There is?" *Geez, lap pools, helicopters, underground bunkers? What else is on this property?*

"We can survey the area from above. It won't take long."

"You can fly a helicopter?" I asked in surprise.

Gabriel nodded. "It's been a while, but flying is like fucking, you never forget how."

I snorted. That sounded like something my best friend, Syd, would say. Before worry about her whereabouts could overwhelm me, I gave Gabriel a hard look. "So neither of you will get out of the helicopter?"

"We don't even have to touch down if you object."

"Good. I very much object." The thought of my lovers being surrounded by zombies made my heart pound. "I don't love the idea, but if you think it's the best course of action..."

"I do," Gabriel said holding my gaze. "We need to know what we are up against."

Ding.

The metal elevator on the far side of the library opened and Mason stepped out. "What's going on?"

"The better question is how are Tina and the kids doing?" I asked, not wanting any more talk of beasts and zombies.

"Very well, considering." He strode over to the desk where we were standing. "Besides a touch of windburn and dehydration they're all in excellent health."

"That's good news." My shoulders sagged with relief. At least we didn't need to worry about zombie kids.

Gabriel scowled at the doctor. "And they had no issues with staying underground?"

Mason shook his head. "The kids are having a ball playing in the game room and Tina crawled into the first bed she found. I don't think she's slept in a week."

"Poor thing. She's been through hell." I gave the young woman massive props for keeping those two kids alive.

"Make sure they stay down there," Gabriel barked to

Mason as he stalked to the door. He looked back at Liam. "Come on."

A panicky feeling came over me. "Wait, you're going now?"

Liam frowned. "I don't like flying."

Gabriel gave him an irritated look. "Don't act like a babe."

"But we haven't had lunch yet." Liam turned his head in the kitchen's direction.

Gabriel huffed the way I used to when Mira was throwing a tantrum. "You can have lunch when we get back. The sooner we leave, the sooner we return."

With a sigh and a quick kiss on my cheek, Liam headed for the door.

Gabriel must've seen the worry on my face. "Don't worry, princess. We'll be back within an hour. Save us some lunch."

"Lots of lunch," Liam added.

"Stay safe," I called after them. My stomach churned as I fought an ominous sense of foreboding. *They'll be fine*, I tried to tell myself.

5

MASON

Havana studied the clock over the double oven, anxiety rolling off her in waves. Although she sat next to me on a bar stool in the kitchen, her focus was on Liam and Gabriel.

I tried for the fourth time to calm my mate. "Relax. They've only been gone thirty minutes."

Havana tightened her fingers around the two-way radio in her hand and brought it up to her mouth. "Liam. Gabriel. Are you okay?"

Static belched out of the device.

I reached across the counter and gently pulled the radio from her hand. "Gabriel said they'd be flying out of range. We'll hear from them shortly."

Her eyes shone with worry. "I don't like this. I don't like this one bit. What if something happens to the helicopter? What if they have to land or—"

"Don't worry." I set down the radio and grabbed her hand in mine. "Even if the worst were to happen, which it won't, those two will be fine." Liam and Gabriel hadn't earned the title of being Tasha's deadliest Enforcers on account of their good looks. The tales of how the two assassins quickly, and often brutally, dispatched Tasha's enemies had reached even my ears at the hospital.

When the two males visited me ten days ago and demanded I come with them, I was sure they'd been sent to kill me. I'd figured Tasha found out I'd gone against her orders. She'd forbidden me from contacting my human family and I'd warned them of the coming outbreak. Since Tasha didn't tolerate disobedience of any kind, I assumed she'd sent her Enforcers after me. It wasn't until we picked Havana up from the strip club that I realized they weren't going to put a bullet in my head.

It was ironic that the males I'd feared would kill me were my new family. We were bound together by our new faction and our bonds to its ruler.

Havana gave me a wan smile and pulled her hand away. "I know, I can't help but worry." Her normally seductive floral scent was awash in fear.

Trying to distract her, I motioned at her untouched meal. "Why don't you eat?"

She looked at her plate and frowned.

"Not a fan of pork?" *Damn, I should have gone with the chicken instead.*

She shook her head. "I'm too worried to eat."

"Can I make you something else?"

"No. I—Thank you for making lunch." She pushed the plate aside. "Can you save it for later?"

"Of course." I'd do absolutely anything for her. If she'd asked me to cut off my arm and charbroil it for her, I would have. My only priority in life was her safety and happiness, and right now she was anything but happy.

I picked up the offending plate making a mental note never to make pork for her again. Knowing that Liam would have no trouble eating Havana's portion, I wrapped it in plastic wrap and put it in the closest fridge. While I was in there, I grabbed a bowl of strawberries and the can of whipped cream. *Now this I know she'll like.*

"Maybe you feel up for these." I shot a little dollop of whipped cream on top and set the bowl down in front of her.

She shook her head. "No, thank you."

My smile faded as I realized her color looked off. "Havana, are you feeling okay?"

She clenched her hands into fists. "No. I feel as if something terrible will happen to Gabriel and Liam."

I started to assure her the guys would be fine, but another look into her worried eyes made me shut my mouth. *What if she's right?* We all had our gifts. Liam had his incredible strength. Gabriel had his speed. I had my empathic and healing abilities. For all I knew Havana's gift could be precognition like Tasha.

Supposedly, the Alpha of Winterhaven often sensed things before they happened. It was one reason she was so hard for assassins to kill. Perhaps when I'd transfused Havana with Tasha's blood, it'd done more than transform her into an Alpha female. *What if she gained Tasha's other abilities?*

I peered into Havana's golden eyes, so different from the deep brown ones she'd had before. In truth, my mate was hardly recognizable from the female we'd rescued a little over a week ago. The angles of her face were sharper, she'd grown several inches in height, and firm muscles had replaced her soft curves. Moreover, Alpha power radiated out of every pore of her body. No Lykos would ever mistake Havana for anything but the Alpha female she was. It was a marvel that a single blood transfusion could bring about such changes.

Blood from an Original like Tasha must hold incredible power. Now that I'd seen how a small amount affected Havana, I wondered if Tasha's blood might be the key to finding a cure for the Z-virus if not for humans, then at least for the young members of our species who lacked the ability to transform and heal themselves.

I'd raided the boxes of medical supplies I'd found in storage and cobbled together a research lab. Unfortunately, although I had several samples of the Z-virus I'd brought with me from the hospital, there were no more bags of Tasha's blood to experiment with.

Every one of my attempts at creating a cure from the blood of other Lykos, had failed. Well, that wasn't entirely true. The resulting antiviral killed the Z-virus, but it also destroyed all the surrounding healthy cells. Tasha's blood might be the answer. If I could only get my hands on more of it...I drummed my fingers on the counter in frustration.

Mistaking my aggravation, Havana reached over and touched my hand. "I really do appreciate you taking a break from your work to make me lunch, hon. You're the best cook. I'm probably the only girl in the apocalypse gaining weight." She let out a husky laugh that made my groin tighten and reminded me it'd been an entire week since we'd been together.

Knowing how fragile the first weeks of pregnancy were for Lykos females, the other males and I had been keeping our distance. Gabriel, Liam, and I even made a pledge not to mate with Havana until the pregnancy was far more established. Finding out she wasn't pregnant was such a relief. The past seven days of refusing her sexual advances had been brutal.

Perhaps it would've been easier if I hadn't already had a taste of her passion. But the memory of her sweet flavor and how wild she went when I drove into her body made sleep impossible. Even ice-cold showers and repeated bouts of self-love did nothing to ease my desperation to have her. And now... knowing she wasn't pregnant, I could finally end my suffering.

A rumbling growl escaped my lips before I could stop it. I looked down at her hand and then back at her mouth. Liam and Gabriel had their fun. *Now it's my turn.* "How much do you appreciate my efforts in the kitchen?"

Her lips curled in a feminine smile. "Very much."

I picked up the can of whipped cream and waved it at her. "Then take that dress off."

Her gaze darted to that damn clock again. "I don't know. Liam and Gabriel—"

"Are fine," I finished. "And you owe me a thank-you."

She chuckled and reached for the belt of her purple dress.

I held my breath as she undid the ties and shrugged off the frock. She wore nothing underneath. *Bloody hell.* The sight of her naked body made my heart skip a beat. Higher level thinking momentarily escaped me as her nipples stiffened in the cool air. How my lips ached to bring those taut peaks into my mouth and then taste the rest of her. Ah, hell the rest of her. She was perfection from the strands of her midnight-black hair to the tips of her toenails.

"You like what you see?"

Incapable of speech, I grunted like that redheaded barbarian. *I hope she's ready for the seven days of pent-up lust I'm about to unleash on her.*

"What now?" Havana asked, her eyes glittering like gemstones.

I pointed at the kitchen island. "Get on the counter," I ordered in my best imitation of Gabriel's gruffness.

Her eyes widened.

She wasn't used to me being domineering, but I'd seen the way she'd responded to Gabriel. There was no question she liked a sexually assertive male and since it was my job to give her everything she wanted... I repeated the order.

"Yes, Doctor." Giving me a sultry look, she sauntered to

the kitchen island. "Are you going to give me a full examination?"

"You'll find out. Get up there," I said, staying in character.

Careful to avoid the pots and pans hanging from a rack overhead, she hopped up on the island. "Ah," she exclaimed.

Dropping the act, I rushed over. "What's wrong?"

"I sat on this," she held up the knife I'd used to cut the stems off the strawberries.

"Are you hurt?" I peered under her thigh.

"I'm fine," she said with a laugh.

"Oh." I laid my palm down on the granite countertop. The slab was freezing. *Well, this won't work.* "We can go somewhere else."

"No, this is perfect." Pushing aside the small mound of strawberry stems, she lay down across the island. "Is this how you want me?"

"Yes," I croaked. She was the most beautiful female I'd ever seen. Remembering my role, I cleared my throat and said, "Now spread your legs."

She complied, baring her rosy pink folds to my hungry gaze.

My penis throbbed to the point of pain. *Bloody hell*, I would not last long once sheathed inside her. *Better make the foreplay good so she doesn't notice my brevity.* I shook the can of whipped cream and coated her left nipple in the white fluff.

She let out a tiny hiss when the cold cream hit her skin, then caught her bottom lip between her teeth.

Christ. I loved it when she did that. Bringing my attention back to her breasts, I leaned over and lapped the sweet cream from her peak.

She moaned. I repeated the action with her right nipple enjoying the way she arched off the counter.

Feeling her mounting excitement and desire through our

bond, I sprayed a trail of cream down her abdomen until I got to the apex of her thighs. There I emptied the can.

"Mason, what are you—"

I shut her up by sucking up the cream on her stomach.

"Oh, my! That feels..."

"Amazing," I finished for her with a grin.

"Sticky."

"What?" I jerked my head up and smacked it on the back of a frying pan. The rest of the hanging pots and pans clanged together.

She giggled. "Are you okay?"

"No," I said batting away the cookware. "You're supposed to be writhing in mindless bliss."

"Like this." She wiggled around.

"Oh, that's it. You'll get it now." Moving away from the blasted pots, I dragged her to the edge of the island where I hooked her legs over my shoulders. Then I buried my head between her thighs.

"Mason!" she shrieked.

"Ah, bloody hell, you taste good." Her musky sweet taste was like ambrosia.

Her moans of ecstasy rang in my ears as I licked her clean.

She thrashed against my lips, begging me to bring her to orgasm.

"Not so fast." I thrust my tongue deep inside her.

She shuddered in response. "Oh, God!"

"No, just Mason," I said cheekily.

She whacked my head with the side of her hand. "Make me come!" She didn't use the Alpha power in her voice, but I was compelled just the same.

Knowing exactly what she needed, I slid two fingers inside and found her G-spot.

"Yes!" she cried, tossing her head back and forth.

Through our bond, I felt her pleasure winding tighter and

tighter until she quivered like a bow. When I knew she couldn't climb any higher, I thrust my fingers inside one more time and suckled hard on her clit.

She shrieked, her entire body seizing. Through our bond, I felt her orgasm crashing into her, obliterating her. So caught up in her emotions, I nearly came in my pants.

No. Inside her. Desperate for release. I ripped open my fly. Then I leaned over the counter and thrust into her with one swift stroke. Her soaking wet heat clamped around my shaft, blinding me with pleasure.

She gave a welcoming moan and locked her ankles around my back.

Daft female. As if I had any intention of ever leaving. Gritting my teeth, I punched my hips trying desperately to take her slowly and make it last.

Undoing all my plans, Havana arched against me and took me deep...so bloody deep. My control snapped.

Feeling more animal than man, I gripped her hips and held her in place. Then I was surging into her hard and fast.

She urged me on with passionate cries. "Yes, Mason! Harder. Faster."

I gave her everything I had until I couldn't hold back anymore. Then I reached between our bodies and found her clit.

She convulsed with a wild, lusty cry.

As her inner muscles clamped down on my cock, I came so intensely I let out a howl that shook the pots and pans above us. Then I collapsed over her. "Have I told you how much I love you?" I said through gulping breaths.

She wrapped her arms around me. "Mason, I lo—"

A loud gasp interrupted her.

Tina stood in the kitchen doorway, a shocked look on her windburned face.

6

HAVANA

Tina's jaw dropped. "You're boning the hot doctor too?"

I felt my face heat as I pushed Mason off me, jumped up, and snatched my dress off the bar stool where I'd left it. *She must think I'm a total slut.* First she found me getting it on with two guys in a cabin and then she walks in on me with yet another man. For a hot minute shame pulsed through me, then I caught her eyeing the muscular perfection of Mason's chest and abs.

Tina moistened her lips, drawing my gaze to her naturally full lips. The young woman was stunning with luminous hazel eyes and a riot of tight blond curls framing her heart-shaped face. Also, without her puffy ski jacket, she had a model-thin build.

Normally, I wasn't the jealous type but the longer she stared at my mate, the angrier I became. *He's mine.* A fierce wave of possessiveness roared through me. A low growl rumbled from my throat. My fingernails lengthened into sharp claws that slashed the dress I was trying to put on.

Tina's gaze snapped to my face. Whatever she saw in my

eyes made her take a step back. She cleared her throat. "I... uh...I'm sorry. That was rude."

"What are you doing up here?" I asked in a sharp voice. Turning to Mason I said, *"Didn't you tell her to stay downstairs?"*

He nodded.

Tina swallowed hard. "I...uh...just wanted to know if you had a spare phone charger? My cell phone is dead." She held up a black phone. "I wanted to check in with my mom."

My irrational anger evaporated as I took in the sheen of tears in her large eyes. "There isn't any cell service. Believe me, I've tried." For the millionth time my thoughts turned to Nathan, Mira, Donna, Max, and Syd. How I hoped against hope they were all alive.

Her shoulders slumped. "I figured as much. I hope she's okay. The last time I talked to my mom she'd just gotten her canine flu vaccine and wasn't feeling well."

I looked over at Mason who was pulling on his pants. *"Doesn't the shot turn people into zombies?"*

The doctor gave a slight nod. *"Best not share that with her right now. I think she's had enough trauma lately."* He yanked his polo shirt over his head.

I secured the belt of my dress and gave the other woman what I hoped was a reassuring smile. "We can still look for a charging cable. There's bound to be one around here somewhere."

"I'd really appreciate that. I hate to ask for more when you've already been so kind to take me and the kids in."

I padded across the tile floor and rested my hand on her shoulder. "We're happy to have you here."

She beamed up at me. Even barefoot, I towered over her. Although it seemed crazy, I could swear I'd grown taller in the past week. It wasn't too obvious when I was with my supersize mates, but standing next to Tina, I felt like a freaking giant.

The girl's eyes brightened. "This place is unreal. I can't believe you still have working electricity. The café lost power the third night."

The reminder of the ski resort had me glancing back at the clock on the wall. The guys had been gone an hour. My stomach knotted and churned. *They should have been back by now.* As I watched the second hand tick across the clock face, a sense of dread grew in the pit of my stomach. My head spun and I lost my balance.

Tina grabbed hold of my arm to keep me from falling. "Are you okay?"

Mason rushed over. "What's wrong?"

I fought to speak through the feeling of impending doom. "Gabriel and Liam…"

"Are those the guys from the cabin?" Tina asked.

Mason nodded. "Yes, they took a helicopter to do a flyover of Sunridge and the ski resort."

Fear choked me as I rushed back to the counter and grabbed the radio. Pressing the talk button I called out, "Liam! Gabriel!"

There was nothing but static.

"Liam!" I tried to reach him through our bond.

There was no response.

The sense that time was running out for my mates intensified. I gave up with a sob. "Mason, they're in trouble, I just know it. If we don't do something…" I couldn't form the words.

Mason wrapped his arms around me. "They'll be okay."

"Stop saying that!" I pushed him away.

He flew into one of the refrigerators.

"Ouch." He turned to inspect the large dent his body had made in the stainless steel door.

Tears burned my eyes. "I'm so sorry, Mason. I keep forgetting my strength." I ran to him and hurled myself into his arms.

Mason rubbed my back. "It's okay. I know you're worried. I'm worried too." He looked over at Tina who was watching us with a look of shock on her face.

Tina's eyes glazed over and her surprised expression faded.

Damn it. I hated that I'd triggered Gabriel's compulsion. *I'll have to be more mindful of how my actions look to humans.*

I took a deep breath and let it out. "We need to figure out where Liam and Gabriel are. Do you think they landed?" I couldn't think of any other reason it'd take them this long to get back.

"They might have," Mason said, looking pensive. "Perhaps they were looking for Nathan and his daughter."

I blinked at the doctor in confusion. "What do you mean?"

Mason pursed his lips and shook his head. "Nathan and Mira were staying at the ski resort until the storm cleared. I thought you knew that."

All the air seemed to leave the room. I struggled to inhale. "No. I didn't know that." *What the hell? All this time they were on the other side of the mountain?*

"If they were staying at the resort, they're dead. Everyone there is dead," Tina said in a hushed voice.

Dead? My knees buckled as a feeling of vertigo came over me.

Mason steadied me before I could fall and gave Tina a hard look. "You're not helping."

Sorry," Tina replied, looking apologetic.

Nathan and Mira are dead? A wild riot of emotions hit me. Confusion. Disbelief. Grief. Memories of happy times we'd spent together flashed in my mind. Playing hide-and-seek with Mira. The feeling of her small arms around my waist and her wet kisses on my cheek. Searing hot nights with Nathan tied to his four-poster bed. The deep rumble in his voice when he told me he loved me. *Oh, God!* It felt as if my rib cage was strangling my heart.

"Take a deep breath," Mason said into my ear. "Good. Now let it out."

Once I'd dragged some oxygen into my lungs, my head stopped spinning and the world sharpened into focus. I straightened my shoulders. "We don't know Nathan and Mira are dead." In fact, I felt somewhere in my gut that they were very much alive. "We need to go search for them and we need to help Gabriel and Liam."

"I don't know if we can. The roads are impassable. Our only option would be hiking down the mountain."

Tina shook her head. "I wouldn't advise that. With all the recent snowfall, there's the potential for avalanches."

There had to be a way of getting down there. "Maybe there's another helicopter in the hangar." Hell, if Tasha had one aircraft, maybe she had another.

Mason shook his head. "I wouldn't know how to fly it if there was. Can you pilot it?"

No. Crap. "Tina, do you know how to fly?"

The young woman shook her head.

A feeling of helpless gripped me. I couldn't just sit here while the people I cared for might be fighting for their lives. "How did you and the kids get here?"

Tina rubbed her hands anxiously. "We took the Midway aerial tram from Snowbird Run to Black Diamond Peak. Then we walked until we saw the mountain road and took it the rest of the way to that cabin of yours."

"How are the trams running without power?" Mason asked her.

"They're solar powered," she answered. "But trust me, you don't want to get anywhere near them. Biters are all over the tram terminals. We lost Josie there." Her expression tightened as if she was relieving the horror of her experience.

I only cared about one thing. "Do the trams go to the resort?"

She nodded, her face pale. "Yes, but it'd be suicide—"

"I'm going."

Mason frowned. "No. You stay here. I'll go help them."

No way was I going to let him go down there alone. I was bigger and stronger than him in wolf form anyway. "We'll both go. If it's as bad as Tina says, Liam and Gabriel will need all the help they can get." *And so will Nathan and Mira.*

Mason opened his mouth as if to argue.

I arched a brow. "Don't make me compel you."

Mason shut his mouth looking slightly aggravated.

"Compel?" Tina's gaze ping-ponged back and forth between me and Mason.

We didn't have time for her questions. We needed to rescue my mates along with Mira. *And Nathan...*

An image of my ex's rugged face wormed its way into my mind. My heart stuttered before finding its rhythm again.

Sensing my thoughts through our bond, Mason searched my face with his beautiful blue eyes. "You still have feelings for Nathan." His tone was resigned not accusatory.

Tina's brows knitted together. "Feelings for who?"

I waved my hand. "Never mind that. How far is the resort from the base tram station?"

She chewed her lower lip. "Not far. The lodge is probably only forty yards from the terminal. It's just past the ticket kiosks. Super easy to get to."

I had a hunch it wouldn't be that easy. "How do we get inside?"

"Um..." She rubbed her hands together anxiously. "There are stairs and an elevator that goes up to the admin offices on the second floor, and the grill on the third floor. There's also a back door that goes into the ski rental and repair shop on the first floor, but the managers keep it locked. Oh, and you can also get in from the skywalk."

"Skywalk?" I echoed.

She nodded. "Yeah, it's the walkway that connects the top floor of the ski lodge to the hotel."

Two buildings. Crap. We'd probably have to search both places. "All right then." I turned to look at Mason. "Are you up for this?"

He nodded slowly. I could tell he was searching for some way to talk me out of it. He wouldn't be able to.

My mind was made up. We would rescue my mates along with Mira and her father. And after everyone was safe, I would give Nathan hell. Then, after I ripped the bastard a new one, I'd decide whether I'd feed him to the zombies. "Let's go now."

"Y-you can't go out there like that," Tina sputtered. "You both need snow gear, and weapons, and—"

"Tina, look at me," I interrupted, infusing my voice with power. I hated using mind control, but there wasn't time for her questions.

She stopped talking and stared at me.

"Once we leave, you'll go downstairs and wait for us to get back. If we don't return by morning, you and the kids can have the run of the place, okay?"

"Okay," she repeated in a monotone voice.

Good. "Now tell us again how to get to the tram."

❦ 7 ❦

LIAM

There were only three things I feared—Tasha, losing Havana, and heights.

As Gabe angled the helicopter forward, I gripped the sides of my seat and closed my eyes. *Fuck. Why did I agree to this? Lykos belong on the ground.* Not squashed into a tiny cockpit like a sardine in a can.

The entire fuselage vibrated along with the spinning blade above our heads. The *whop whop whop* sound bore into my skull like a flock of frenzied woodpeckers.

Havana's voice came through the radio in my hand. "Liam, are you okay?" Her anxious tone had me snapping my eyes open.

Gabe gave me a chastising look. *"She's picking up on your fear through the bond, brother."* He snatched the radio out of my hand and said, "Liam is fine, princess. We've barely gotten off the ground. Now remember, we're flying out of range so we'll lose contact for a little while."

"Okay," she said in a breathless voice. "Just be careful up there."

I grabbed the radio from Gabe. "We will, beautiful. You tell Doc to keep my lunch warm."

I waited for her response, but there was only the crackle of static. Disappointed, I set the radio down.

Gabe shook his head.

"What?"

His dark eyes narrowed. "You need to get your shit together and stop acting like a cowardly pup."

What the fuck? "Call me a coward again," I snarled. Despite Gabe being the Head Enforcer of Winterhaven, my body count was easily double his. Maybe he needed to be reminded of that fact. I clenched my hands into fists.

Gabe bared his teeth and moved the lever between his legs.

The helicopter pitched to the side.

Screaming, I braced my hands against the ceiling of the helicopter. "Ah fucking hell. Stop that!"

Gabe had the nerve to laugh as he righted the aircraft. "You should see yourself. I think you were close to pissing your pants."

Forgetting my fear of heights for the moment, I grinned. It'd been ages since I'd heard Gabe's deep rumbling chuckle. He hadn't so much as told a joke or cracked a smile in years. Not since Tasha ordered him to murder his entire family. *And who can blame him?* The male had literally lived everyone's worst nightmare. I never thought he'd recover from it. But then Havana had come along.

She'd healed Gabe physically and emotionally. For that I'd be eternally grateful. Not that I wasn't already eternally grateful to her for choosing me as her mate.

My spirits rose higher than the fucking chopper. Havana had bonded with me! Me. Liam the Skull Crusher. No longer would I be the unchosen giant that females, both Lykos and human, backed away from in fear.

The stupid grin on my face faded as the memories of watching other males be chosen over me time after time flashed into my mind. Before the familiar hurt could take root, I pushed it away. It didn't matter anymore. They didn't matter anymore. It was Havana and me now. Well... technically me, Gabe, Doc, and Havana now. But I didn't mind sharing.

I looked over at Gabe who was staring straight ahead.

"That's something you don't see every day," he said pointing out the windshield.

I followed his gaze and grunted. It was a nice view if you were into snowy mountain ranges and pine trees that looked like rock candy lollipops reaching up to the sky. *Mmm. Lollipops.* My stomach rumbled reminding me it'd been hours since I'd last eaten. Before we'd left, I caught a whiff of what Doc had been cooking. Pork chops. My favorite. I rubbed my belly wishing Gabe would turn the flying death trap around.

"There's the ski resort," Gabe said nodding at the cluster of buildings appearing in the distance.

I glanced down at the empty ski lifts. I didn't see a single zombie anywhere. *Where are all the undead?*

"Probably buried under the snow," Gabe answered, reading my mind. "That's the hotel, and that's the lodge," he added, flying the chopper straight toward two buildings. The taller modern square building had to be the hotel. It connected to the more rustic-looking ski lodge via a glass-enclosed walkway.

Motion inside the walkway caught my attention. "Are there people in there?"

"Not sure. Let's get a closer look." Gabe did a slow flyover.

There was a shark frenzy of bloody bodies inside the glass tube. All were slamming themselves against the door leading to the ski lodge. It didn't take more that a heartbeat to realize those things were zombies. There was only one reason they'd be trying to take down the door.

Gabe cursed, coming to the same conclusion. "There are survivors in the lodge."

Fuck. I clenched my hands into fists. "What do we do?"

Before Gabe could respond, a deep voice boomed inside my mind. *"Thank the fates you're here."*

Gabe stiffened, obviously hearing the same voice. *"Nathan, are you inside the lodge?"*

Nathan? As in Nathan Steele, the Alpha?

Gabe nodded his head slightly in response to my unspoken question.

"Yes. What the fuck took you so long?" The Alpha's voice carried a mixture of relief and anger. *"I'm here with Mira and nearly a dozen human survivors. Look to your left."*

Gabe and I looked over at the ski lodge.

The silver-haired male leaned out a window and waved at us. Even from this distance I could see lines of tension on the Alpha's face and dark red stains covering his dress shirt. *What the hell happened to him?*

A small female face appeared in the window next to Nathan. Based on the child's long, silver-streaked hair, it had to be his daughter, Mira.

On one hand, I was happy the young Alpha female had survived, but on the other, I sensed bringing her and Nathan back to Sanctuary would complicate things. I didn't like complications.

I knew Gabe hadn't searched for the Alpha male, up until now, for the exact same reason.

Gabe glanced at the two seats behind us. *"We won't be able to fit everyone."*

"Then we'll take trips." Nathan said in an authoritative tone. *"The children go first."*

Children? My gut twisted. I hated the thought of any child in danger.

Gabe didn't miss a beat. *"We can fly them to Sanctuary and come back for the rest."*

"We have to hurry. I don't know how long the skywalk door will hold. Can you land on top of the lodge?" Nathan asked.

"Negative," Gabe responded looking at the pitched roof. *"What about the parking lot in front?"*

"That's a no-go. I've barricaded the Ackermans downstairs, but if you land on the ground, there's a chance they'll get out and attack you."

"Who are the Ackermans?"

"Think super fast zombies that regenerate injuries," replied Nathan. *"Trust me. You don't want to run into them."*

Fast zombies? I didn't like the sound of that.

"How many Ackermans are there?" Gabe asked.

"Two. Paul and Linda are nearly impossible to kill and they're not dumb like the other zombies. They've come close to dismantling the barricade twice." The tightness in Nathan's voice betrayed the danger he and the other survivors were in.

"It's a good thing we came along when we did," I said privately to Gabe.

Gabe nodded and turned his attention to the hotel. *"What if I landed there?"* He flew the chopper to a large hotel balcony overlooking the skywalk. It looked as if the balcony belonged to the hotel's restaurant. Snow-covered tables and chairs were stacked near French patio doors, leaving a wide-open space to land the chopper.

I sent the Alpha a mental image of the location.

"That'll work. I'll carry the children over the skywalk, and hand them up to you. Stand by." Nathan broke off the connection with us.

Gabe slowly lowered the chopper down. The whirling rotor blade turned the snow on the balcony into a mini blizzard around us.

We both held our breaths as the landing skids touched down. When it didn't seem as if the balcony would collapse, I unbuckled my harness and started to open the door.

"Wait for the blade to stop," yelled Gabe.

"Fuck that. You keep the chopper running. We may need to fly out of here at a moment's notice." I jumped out of the cockpit, and then keeping my head ducked down, I ran to the railing on the edge of the balcony. From there I could make out Nathan climbing out of the ski lodge window.

Displaying enviable strength, the silver-haired Alpha male pulled himself onto the roof with one arm. Besides his blood-stained shirt, he wore a pair of shredded dress pants that looked as if they'd gone through a shift. He had something strapped to his chest. It took me a second to realize it was an infant.

Ah hell.

While I was digesting the fact that we would need to care for a tiny babe, Nathan braced one arm on the roof and reached the other arm down.

A gray-haired human female appeared in the window. She helped a young boy, around the age of five, climb out.

The Alpha grabbed the boy and maneuvered him onto his back. Once the boy's hands locked around his neck, Nathan reached down to the window.

The old woman was already lifting his daughter up toward him. Tendrils of the girl's silver-streaked hair flew around her face.

Nathan grabbed Mira, secured her on his left hip, and reached down to the window again.

Fuck. How many babes are there?

This time the human handed him a toddler dressed in a blue snowsuit.

After snatching up the toddler, the Alpha male stood. With the toddler in his right arm, his daughter in his left, the older boy on his back, and the infant strapped to his chest, Nathan carefully made his way across the sloping ski lodge roof toward the skywalk.

My blood iced over as I watched his slow progress.

When he finally reached the skywalk, he shouted, "Do you have a rope?"

I realized there was at least a dozen feet between the top of the skywalk and the balcony. In wolf form, the Alpha could have easily covered that distance, but there was no way he could shift with the precious cargo he carried.

"We need rope!" I mentally shouted at Gabe.

"There's some in the back."

Ducking to avoid the lethal blade, I ran to the chopper door and wrenched it open.

"There," Gabe said, motioning at a coil of thick rope strapped to the back of his seat.

I quickly uncoiled it, secured one end to the landing skids, and then ran back to the balcony railing.

Below, Nathan was slowly crossing the top of the skywalk. His bare foot knocked free a large clump of snow that tumbled three stories down.

The zombies inside the walkway frantically slapped and punched at the glass, following Nathan's progress like fish in an aquarium. As more and more dead crammed into the small space, spiderweb fractures appeared in the walls.

Oh fuck. The skywalk is not going to hold.

"Where's my rope?" Nathan shouted.

I tossed the end of the rope over the rails.

Nathan shifted the toddler and grabbed the rope. Then he tied it around the little guy's waist. "Bring him up!"

The toddler started wailing as soon as Nathan released him to dangle in the air.

I leaned over the balcony and reeled the babe in.

As soon as I had him, the chubby-cheeked tyke stopped crying.

"It's okay, little man," I said, in a gentle voice, setting him down. Feeling bad that I didn't have time to comfort the toddler, I threw the rope back over the side of the balcony.

This time Nathan tethered his daughter.

It looked as if she was fighting him. "No, Daddy. I'm staying with you."

"Sunshine, go with Liam and Gabriel. They'll take you to Vana. Then they'll come back for me."

"Vana?" Mira's voice shook.

More cracks formed along the side of the walkway.

"Hurry!" I shouted.

Bloodcurdling shrieks rang out.

For a moment I thought the babe strapped to Nathan was wailing, but then I caught sight of two shrieking figures racing around the side of the building. One was a tall, lanky male dressed in flannel boxer shorts. The other was a voluptuous dark-haired naked woman whose quivering breasts captivated me for a moment.

Nathan looked down at them and paled. *"Those are the Ackermans!"* Moving frantically he unbuckled the baby carrier around his waist and fastened it around Mira. "Hold on tight to baby Sierra."

Looking dazed, Mira clutched the babe to her chest.

The infant began to cry. Her tiny shrieks melded in with the otherworldly cries of the Ackermans.

Below the skywalk, the dark-haired woman unhinged her jaw and let out another shriek that rattled my skull. Then she bent her knees and jumped on top of the walkway, landing a few yards from Nathan.

They can jump???

"Bring them up!" Nathan shouted, and then he spun around to face the woman.

Instead of attacking, the naked woman sank down on her haunches studying Nathan and the child clinging to his neck.

The hair on the back of my neck rose. *What the fuck is she?* Not sure I wanted to find out, I yanked Mira and the wailing babe up lightning fast. Then I quickly untied them and set them down on the balcony next to the toddler.

One more to go. "Here!" I tossed the rope over the rails.

Nathan carefully swung the boy off his back and reached for the rope.

"Mom!" shouted the boy. He ducked between Nathan's legs, making a beeline for the naked woman.

"No, Kaden!" Nathan darted after the boy and grabbed him. "She's not your mom anymore."

The woman gnashed her blood-covered teeth.

That's the kid's mother? Shit. "Tether him! I'll bring him up!"

Nathan tightened his arms around the boy.

The child was fighting him. Even though his mother was clearly anything but human, the young fool still wanted to go to her.

"You have to go with Liam." With his arms wrapped tightly around the kicking boy, the Alpha male turned toward the rope.

In a blur of motion, the woman sprang into the air and slammed into Nathan's back. Nathan and the boy flew off the top of the walkway. Thankfully, a thick snowbank broke their fall.

Just as I released a relieved breath, the naked woman let out another shriek and followed them to the ground. Immediately she and the tall male started circling Nathan and the boy like hungry sharks.

Fuck!

Nathan ripped the boy out of the snow and backed toward the wall.

He needs my help! "Nathan!" I slung a leg over the rail,

preparing to jump down and assist.

The Alpha male glanced up at me. "Liam, go now! Get the kids to safety!" His shout carried so much Alpha power, it made my head ring.

Damn him! Unable to fight Nathan's compulsion, I gathered the children and carried them to the chopper.

As I jumped in back with the babes, Gabe spun around. "What's going on?"

"Nathan's in trouble," I said through gritted teeth. "But he compelled me to take these kids and go." Needing to secure the children, I set Mira and the babe in the seat next to mine and buckled the shoulder lap belt across their small bodies. Not knowing what else to do with the toddler, I pulled him into my lap with his face pressed against my chest.

The little guy clung to me like a monkey, blinking up at me with thickly lashed brown eyes.

Nathan's compulsion drove me to shout, "Why aren't we moving? Let's go!"

Gabe whistled. "You don't see that every day."

I followed his gaze out the side window.

The naked female stood perched on the balcony railing staring at us.

Fuck! I didn't know what she was capable of, but based on Nathan's fear of her, I didn't want to find out. "Get us in the air, Gabe!"

Gabe spun around to the flight deck and seconds later we rose into the air. Suddenly, we pitched to the side.

"What's happening?" I yelled, buckling the seat harness around the toddler and me.

"You didn't untie the rope!" Gabe shouted.

"What?" I looked out the window.

The naked female was underneath us, yanking hard on the trailing rope still attached to the helicopter's landing skids. *Oh, shit!*

❧ 8 ❧

HAVANA

The dread swirling in the depths of my stomach intensified as Mason and I bounded over the Sanctuary walls in wolf form.

We raced past the cabin, neither of us even sparing the small building a glance. Following Tina's instructions we stayed on the road until we came to a small bridge. There, we veered west following a frozen river for a few miles until we came to a thick forest of trees.

Branches clawed at my fur as we raced by a sign designating the area as part of the Sunridge ski resort. *We have to be getting close.* We switched directions and headed north.

It felt wrong to head up the mountain, but according to Tina there was no quicker way down the mountain than the trams that traveled from summit to base.

Panting, Mason and I climbed until the pine trees abruptly disappeared and we found ourselves on a large mountain peak. We ran to the east side of the summit and looked down. Below us was a wide steep slope, dotted with jagged rocks jutting out of the snow.

"Look there." Mason pointed his snout at the cables in the

distance. The black cables—hanging dozens of feet off the ground, were stark against the gray sky. It looked as if they'd been strung from the bottom of the mountain, through several lattice steel towers, straight to a large metal structure up ahead.

Mason slowed. *"That has to be the tram terminal."*

Finally! "Let's go." I bolted over to the structure only to find an empty platform. *"Where's the tram?" It has to be here.* Panic clogged my throat. *"Where's the goddamn tram?"*

Mason followed close behind. *"Just relax, love. It's on its way."* He looked up at the moving haul cable and the whirling gears above our heads. *"Remember Tina said there are two trams that run continuously."*

"Right." Tina also said the tram terminals had been packed with zombies. *Crap.* Anxiety chewed at me while we waited. Unable to sit calmly like the golden wolf next to me, I paced in a circle.

"It's here," Mason announced, his gaze fixed on the green-and-silver boxlike tram moving toward us. *"Remember the plan."*

I nodded. My stomach knotted as I settled into position next to him. Every muscle in my body coiled, ready to pounce on whatever dead thing walked out.

The tram swung into the platform and stopped. The double doors slid open.

My heart hammered and my breath came in jagged pants.

Nothing stumbled out. Nothing moved inside.

Slowly the tension seeped out of my body. *Maybe it really isn't as bad as Tina says.*

"Wait here," Mason ordered, before cautiously approaching the doors.

I rolled my eyes. *When will he and the others get that I'm the Alpha?* Growling, I bounded past Mason and dove into the tram.

The smell of rotting meat slapped me in the face. My

paws slid on the sticky, wet floor and I skidded straight into something soft and squishy. A quick look down made bile rise up the back of my throat. I was standing inside the remains of someone—an almost entirely eaten someone.

"Serves you right for not waiting," Mason said, stepping into the tram.

Letting out a soft whine, I tried to shake my paws free of the viscera, and nearly tripped over the dead person's legs. Based on the length of the jagged, fully exposed, femur, the deceased had been an adult male. *Oh, Jesus. There are teeth marks in the bone.* My stomach rolled. Against my better judgment, I looked at the guy's face. It, and most of the dead guy's head, was missing.

Mason looked at the blood-smeared floor. *"It's not as bad as I expected."*

Gagging on the rancid stench, I gave him a WTF look.

"It's better if you breathe through your mouth," Mason advised.

Finding that mouth breathing helped, I scanned the tram. The inside was surprisingly large—nearly as big as my old apartment bedroom. There were no seats though. Based on the straps dangling from the ceiling, riders were supposed to stand.

Not wanting to risk sliding into the bloody carcass again, I shifted into my human form and grabbed the nearest strap.

Following my lead, Mason shifted too.

As we stood in silence, my anxiety rose. *Did we make the right call in not bringing weapons?*

Reading my mind, Mason slid his arm around my bare shoulder and pulled me into his chest. "As wolves we'll be much faster than the reanimated and our claws and teeth will shred their decaying flesh."

"And we can heal any injuries we get by shifting?"

"That's right." He kissed the top of my head. "As long as we don't get trapped by a horde of them, we'll be fine."

I stiffened. "What happens if we get trapped by a horde?"

"Best to not think of that. Just remember to incapacitate the brains of the reanimated. It's the only way to stop them."

"Take out their brain. Got it," I stated with false confidence. *How the hell are we going to do that in wolf form?*

The doors slid closed with a metallic clang and the tram rocked forward.

The sudden propulsion threw me off-kilter.

Mason tightened his arms around me, holding me in place. "To keep your center of gravity, keep your knees slightly bent and your feet wide."

"Or I could just cling to you," I said, giving him a quick kiss. There was much I could learn from my Omega like how he could remain calm when we were hurling into a potential nightmare.

Trying to channel some inner-Mason, I took a deep breath and looked out the window. Although the views of the snow-laden trees and pristine white ski slopes should have eased my anxiety, they didn't. The gray sky was darkening. Soon the sun would set leaving us to battle the dead in the black of night.

Fighting back a shiver, I turned my attention to the strange holes dotting the slopes. Some holes were wide enough to crawl through while others were barely softball-sized. *Weird.* I squinted to get a better look at one. The hole grew wider under my gaze. A glove-covered hand emerged briefly only to be swallowed by more shifting snow.

Oh, God. Those are zombies. They were buried right now, but when the snow melted... A sick feeling gripped me. "Mas—"

He cursed, his attention fixed on the front window.

I followed his gaze and my stomach fell to the floor. The next tram terminal, along with another large building, was visible in the distance. They teemed with zombies.

From this vantage point, the dead looked like swarms of

colorful ants crowding around the platform. *Shit! When the tram doors open, they'll all rush in.* "Mason, what do we do?"

"First, we take a deep breath and let it out." Mason inhaled and exhaled audibly. "Remember we anticipated this. We just need to stop the doors from opening." He strode over to the doors and ran his hands down the side of each one. "There has to be some kind of mechanism here."

We were getting closer to the terminal. The lurching figures were recognizable now. Most wore blood-covered ski apparel; some dragged half-eaten limbs behind them. "Did you find it?"

"No." There was a hint of anxiety in his voice. It was enough to push my panic button.

I searched the small space for some kind of solution, my gaze coming to rest on the bloody carcass. *Oh, crap. That's how we'll end up.*

"I'll keep looking," Mason said, turning his attention back to the doors. "Maybe if we could find something to wedge in here."

"What about the guy's femur?" I pointed at the floor.

Mason shook his head. "I need something longer like a ski or a ski pole. Bloody hell. Why couldn't someone have left one aboard?" He smacked the door.

The station was only a hundred yards away. Several zombies on the platform were lifting their heads and sniffing the air. *Can they smell us?* "Mason! We're almost there."

He clenched his jaw. "Okay, here's plan B. When the doors open, I'll run out—"

"No!" I shouted.

He continued. "I'll run out and try to get them to follow me. You'll continue the rest of the way by yourself, and I'll meet you at the bottom."

"You'll be torn apart. There has to be another way. Don't

these things come with emergency exits? I mean even elevators have an opening on top."

We both looked up at the ceiling at the same time. Between the dangling straps was the outline of a hatch.

"You're bloody brilliant." Mason moved underneath the hatch. He reached up, but wasn't tall enough to reach it.

"Here!" I rushed over and picked him up. Despite his tall, muscular build, his weight barely registered.

He let out a sound of surprise. "Havana—"

"Swallow your manly pride and open that damn hatch." My voice rose as the tram began to slow. We were just feet from the terminal.

Mason fumbled with the hatch.

"Hurry!"

The tram came to a stop.

In a scene straight out of a horror movie, dozens of zombies in brightly colored ski jackets surrounded the tram on all sides. Their grotesque, rotting faces smeared the glass. The tram shuddered under their beating fists. One window by the door shattered. A sea of rotting hands reached inside.

Oh, God! We'll die in here! "Mason!"

"I can't get it. It's stuck!" Panic, anger, and grief thrummed through our bond.

Refusing to accept our grim fate, I set Mason down. Then I bent my knees and jumped upward with my fist outstretched. Using every bit of my strength, I punched straight through the hatch sending the square piece of metal flying over the side of the car and into the mass of rioting dead. My knuckles screamed in agony, but there wasn't time for pain.

The tram doors whooshed open. The zombie horde tried to rush in but there were too many of them crushing together. For a brief moment, none could get through.

I grabbed Mason and all but threw him through the

hatch. Then I jumped after him. I'd barely pulled myself up on the roof when the tram filled with putrid-smelling zombies.

"Bloody hell," Mason shouted over the chorus of clicking teeth and clunking ski boots.

As my adrenaline crashed, I collapsed next to him, cradling my throbbing right hand. It was probably broken in at least three places.

Mason reached for my hand. "Let me look."

"There's no need." To prove my point, I shifted into a wolf and back. The pain vanished. "Look, good as new," I held up my healed hand for him to inspect.

He gave me a tight smile. "Well. That's one problem solved. What do we do about them?" He motioned down.

Dozens of milky-white eyes stared up at us from faces in varying states of decay. Some bloated faces were a mottled purplish-blue color, while others were as white as spider eggs and covered in dense black veins. All of their lips were black and drawn back to expose their chattering bloody teeth.

The clicking sound made my skin crawl. "Why are they doing that?"

"I don't know. But if they don't move out of the tram, it's not going anywhere."

To prove his words, the tram doors started to close. As soon as they hit the zombies trying to cram their way inside, the doors retracted.

Crap. I scanned the area looking for some kind of solution and found none. The building next to the terminal offered only more zombies. Through the broken windows, I could see the dead stumbling over chairs and lurching into tables. At least the creatures weren't too bright. *If we could only distract them with something...*

Mason nodded as if I'd spoken out loud. "Back to plan B

then. I'll draw them away from the tram." He stood and walked to the edge of the roof.

"No!" I scrambled after him and grabbed his arm. "I'm not letting you commit suicide."

He cracked a smile. "While I would gladly sacrifice my life for yours, if I die, you die, remember?"

"Oh, yeah." When I first bonded with my mates, they'd explained how we'd tied our life forces together. I didn't pretend to understand the mechanics of it, but I trusted the guys at their word. It gave even more urgency to our current mission. If we didn't save Liam and Gabriel, and they ended up dying, so would we.

Mason rotated his arms around as if loosening them. "Once I've outrun the dead, I'll head the rest of the way down the mountain on foot."

"On paws you mean," I corrected.

"Right," he said with a wry grin. "You take the tram down and I'll meet you at the base tram terminal."

Before I could argue that I should be the one to jump out since I was bigger and faster, he shifted and dove over the side of the tram.

Heart in my throat, I watched him run several yards away from the platform. Then he stopped and let out a long, loud howl.

Every zombie in the vicinity stopped and turned toward him.

"It's working! They're going after you." I peered down at the emptying tram.

Mason howled again.

Zombies lurched toward him, moving closer and closer.

Fear climbed up the back of my throat. "They're surrounding you!"

A short male zombie in a red ski jacket grabbed for him.

Mason darted back just in time. *"I got this. Don't worry about me."*

Below me, the tram doors closed and moments later the empty car swung forward. Nearly losing my footing, I grabbed the thick metal bar that connected the car to cables above.

A war raged inside me. *Do I jump down and help Mason or stay to find the others?*

The tram picked up speed, and the decision was made for me. As Mason faded from view I shouted, "Please don't die!"

He didn't respond.

❧ 9 ❧

NATHAN

The ravenous dead pounded against the cracking glass walls of the skywalk above my head, but I didn't dare tear my gaze from Paul Ackerman's unblinking silver eyes.

Paul watched us with preternatural stillness.

His son, Kaden, trembled behind me, his teeth chattering in the icy wind. The human boy was no doubt freezing with only a thin jacket to protect him from the elements, but his parents presented a far greater threat to his life than hypothermia right now.

Damn the fates. After watching our chances of survival fade with every hour, I'd thought Gabriel and Liam's arrival meant our luck had finally turned.

Mira, myself, and the humans I'd rescued were running dangerously low on food, but I refused to let anyone leave our stronghold on the third floor after what happened to the Ackermans. Seven days ago, Paul and Linda left to scavenge for food and had been killed.

I didn't know how or why, but they had reanimated into something far more threatening than the shambling dead.

Their speed, stealth, and the way they hunted as a pack had reduced our survivor group by half and nearly cost me my life.

Paul cocked his head to the side and studied me with an intensity that made my hair stand on end. His musty scent was definitely not Lykos and certainly not human. His formerly olive-toned skin held a grayish cast, and I knew from experience he possessed enough strength to rip a man apart with his bare hands. He wasn't alone. Despite Linda's size, she too was incredibly powerful. She might even be strong enough to pull a helicopter out of the sky.

I spared a quick glance up at the hotel balcony railing where Linda stood, a coil of rope in her clawed hand. *Why hadn't the Enforcers cut the fucking rope?* A sliver of fear arrowed down my spine.

Gabriel and Liam will handle it, I told myself. I'd never imagined a day would come where I'd put Mira's life in the hands of Tasha's brute squad. But I was out of options and so was Kaden. If I left the boy to challenge his mother, his father would kill him. *I can't let that happen.* I shifted my gaze back to Paul.

He let out an earsplitting shriek and sank back into a crouch.

Fuck! I'd been giving my rations to the other survivors, which greatly depleted my strength. However, I'd be damned if I showed the creature an inch of weakness. I threw my head back and howled.

Kaden let out a shocked cry and released his death grip on my leg.

Damnation. I can't have the boy scared of me. I turned and stared into the boy's wide brown eyes. "Kaden, you will not be afraid and you will stay with me when I turn into a wolf."

My compulsion did its job. The expression of terror on the boy's face faded. He nodded, his eyes glassy.

I stood protectively in front of him and turned to face

Paul. Although I was an Alpha, I knew my chance of defeating Paul, who regenerated any injury instantly, were slim to none. Nevertheless, I had to try for the boy's sake. Moving quickly, I tore off my clothing and shifted.

Paul didn't so much as blink when my bones lengthened, tendons snapped, and fur sprouted over my rippling muscles.

Rising as a large silver wolf, I snarled at him.

Paul gnashed his bloody teeth and looked up at Linda as if awaiting her command.

I lowered myself to the ground. *"Climb on,"* I telepathically ordered the boy.

Although humans normally couldn't receive Lykos thoughts, Kaden did, reinforcing my suspicion that the family wasn't entirely human. Slinging his legs over my back, the little boy grabbed hold of my fur.

"Hang on!" As soon as I knew the boy was secure. I took off.

Snarling, Paul bolted after us.

Fuck! He's fast.

Paul stayed right on my heels, his fetid breath stinking the air.

My lungs burned as I raced around the side of the hotel through the parking lot. Veering around the mounds of snow I knew were cars, I tried to formulate a plan.

Where do I take Kaden? The hotel was filled with zombies and so was the first floor of the ski lodge, but we couldn't stay out in the open. In the distance I spied a tram swinging into the base terminal. *Thank the fates!*

For a week we'd watched the tram come and go up the mountain, but any survivor who made a run for it had met their bloody end at the hands of the Ackermans. I hadn't dared risk Mira's life to get to it and I refused to leave her behind. Now the tram might be Kaden's only chance. I just needed to get him inside and then keep his father distracted while he escaped. Setting my sights on the terminal, I increased my pace.

Kaden flattened himself over my back, his small boots digging into my ribs.

Just past the ticket kiosks the snow deepened. It took more and more energy to push my way through. *Damnation.*

Paul was gaining on me.

I kept my gaze locked on the tram terminal. The tram was still in the dock, but I had to hurry. *If it leaves, we're fucked!* Summoning my waning strength, I forced myself to run even faster. My lungs burned, my breath sawed in and out.

Almost there! We were close enough that I could make out the tram's blood-smeared windows. It looked empty. Thank the fates. If I could just get the boy inside—

Something moved on the roof of the tram.

I blinked.

A naked female rose from a crouch. As she looked out at me her long dark hair whipped around a beautiful face I knew better than my own.

Vana? It can't be. I stumbled.

Something heavy slammed into my side.

Fuck!

Kaden flew off my back and landed in the snow a dozen feet away.

Paul pinned me face-first to the ground.

I tried to shake him off, but the bastard dug his claws into my hide and buried his jaws into the back of my neck. A pained yelp tore from my lips as Paul ripped out a large chunk of my flesh.

Searing agony radiated from the wound. *Have to get him off.* I bucked hard and threw him.

Paul landed on his feet, chewing noisily. A line of crimson streamed down his chin and bare chest. Over his shoulder I could see the tram. The roof was empty.

I shook my head trying to clear the black dots in my line of vision. *Did I hallucinate Vana?* Blood poured from my throbbing wound.

"Daddy, stop!" Kaden cried.

Paul and I jerked our head in his direction.

The boy stared at his father, my compulsion making him too brave for his own good.

"Run!" I telepathically ordered. *"Go to the tram! Get inside!"*

The boy took off toward the terminal.

Paul started to follow.

I forced myself to my feet and leaped in front of the undead creature. *Have to protect the boy.* Digging into the last of my reserves, I shifted to human and back to wolf. Instead of completely regenerating, my wound only partially healed. There was no time to acknowledge what that meant.

Paul let out an inhuman roar and lunged for me.

I jumped to meet him in midair—a hundred and seventy pounds of super zombie crashing into two hundred pounds of Alpha male.

This time I snapped my jaws around his throat. His bitter-tasting blood filled my mouth making me gag. I forced my teeth in deeper.

Seeming impervious to the bite, Paul locked his arms around my torso and squeezed so hard and fast that my spine snapped with an audible crack.

My back exploded in pain and my limbs went numb. Unable to move my front or back paws, I panicked. Releasing his throat, I gnashed at his arms, chest, and neck with my teeth.

He flung me away.

I landed in a broken heap of gut-wrenching pain. I tried to shift and failed.

Paul let out a victorious shriek.

Darkness encroached on my vision. I fought it. *Have to*

save the boy. I tried again to shift. I couldn't. My lungs filled with blood. I fought to drag in a gulp of air.

Paul stalked over, his eerie silver eyes gleaming.

Damn the fates. This is it. The fiend would end me. I'd never be reunited with Vana. I'd never see my daughter grow up. *Worse my failure would cost the boy his life.*

Paul opened his jaws monstrously wide.

I refused to flinch as death prowled closer.

Inches away, Paul suddenly froze. Something jagged and white burst through the center of his forehead. Paul opened and closed his mouth, then collapsed.

What the hell?

Vana stepped around his fallen body. "Nathan! Are you okay?"

I gaped at the sight of her.

She was even more beautiful than I remembered. Her golden skin seemed to glow against the ivory snow as she knelt by my side. *She's a hallucination. I must be dying.*

"The child is safe—he's waiting at the tram terminal. I killed all the zombies there." Vana's warm hands cupped my muzzle. "You have to shift and heal yourself, Nathan."

I wanted to respond, but couldn't. I lacked even the strength to lift my head.

A golden wolf ran to Vana's side. A split second later, it shifted into Mason.

Vana turned to him, tears running down her face. "Thank God you made it, Mason. Nathan isn't shifting. Do something!"

The doctor stared silently down at me.

I refused to tear my gaze from Vana. I wanted the last thing I saw to be her face.

Mason shook his head. "There's nothing I can do. Do you want to say goodbye?"

"Goodbye? You mean—" she made a choking sound.

"Damn it, Nathan. You have to shift!" Tears swam in her brilliant gold eyes.

That's not right. Vana has brown eyes. My mind must be playing tricks on me. I wanted to look again, but my eyelids were too heavy to keep open. I burned with the need to tell her how much I loved her. A buzzing noise distracted me.

Vana held my head in her lap and stroked my fur. "I can't lose him, Mason. I can't."

How I wanted to ease her pain. I never wanted her to suffer on account of me.

"There may be a way to save him," Mason said softly. "If you bonded with him, you could give him some of your strength. It might be enough for him to shift."

Vana sniffed. "But he could still die. You said if one bonded mate dies, they all die."

The buzzing sound grew louder making it harder to follow their conversation.

Mason let out a deep breath. "True. But I've also seen it where one mate kept the other alive, akin to a lifeline. You'd have to decide whether to risk it."

No! I didn't want her to risk her life. I tried to reach her mind telepathically, but the buzzing in my head blocked me.

Vana sobbed. *"But—"*

"He doesn't have more than a minute, Havana."

The buzzing now sounded like voices. It'd been decades since I'd heard my parents. *Mama? Papa?* A strong pulling sensation lifted my consciousness. I let out one last labored breath. Then I floated toward the voices. Toward the light.

"Nathan Steele, you will not die. I order you to bond to me!" The power in Vana's voice dragged me back to my body.

"You're mine!" she said. "Say you're mine."

"I am yours," I whispered. A soul-deep connection snapped between us. Energy from her life force raced through our bond, strengthening me.

"Now shift!" she ordered.

The shift, one of the most painful of my life, took an agonizing minute and left me panting, still paralyzed in my human form. Stunned with the impossibly of it all, I laid dazed in the snow staring up at her.

"You're mine!" she said again, leaning over me.

"Always," I gasped, feeling her worry, her fear, and her love. It was that last emotion I focused on as the last of my energy ebbed and I sank into oblivion.

HAVANA

Panic beat inside my chest as Nathan's eyes rolled back. "Is he—" I couldn't even say the words.

"Relax. He's unconscious. Not dead." Mason put a hand on my shoulder. "He should be fine after some rest. You did it. You saved his life."

I let out a deep breath. *I'd claimed him. Nathan is my mate.* I couldn't wrap my head around that. Everything happened so fast.

From the top of the tram I'd seen Nathan trying to protect a child from that thing, whatever it was. I looked over at the lifeless creature I'd staked in the head with the femur. Whatever it was, it had to be very powerful to take down Nathan.

When I saw Nathan fall all my anger and bitterness had been swept away by grief. In that moment, I knew I had to save him and the child I'd thought was Mira.

I peered at the tram terminal where I'd compelled the boy to stay. *Where's Mira?* I looked down at Nathan wishing I could ask him.

"Maybe she's in the helicopter with Gabriel and Liam," Mason said, reading my mind.

I looked up at the sky. "I don't see the helicopter."

Mason's brows drew together. "It was just there—"

A thunderous crash sounded.

We both twisted in the hotel's direction. Smoke billowed from the skywalk.

My bonds with Liam and Gabriel exploded in intense pain. "Oh, God! No!" I had to go to them.

"Keep Nathan and the boy safe!" I ordered Mason. Then I shifted into a wolf and ran straight toward the clouds of black smoke. *"Liam! Gabriel!"*

Neither male responded.

Anguish threatened to overwhelm me. *No. If I'm still here, they're still here.* Pushing the negative emotions away, I bounded toward the hotel and lodge. My legs nearly gave out when I spied the wreckage of the helicopter between the two buildings.

The mangled machine looked as if it had sideswiped the skywalk before slamming nose down into a deep snowdrift. From this vantage point, the helicopter looked like a broken toy with the tail snapped half-off. Somehow the smoking main rotor still spun, churning clumps of snow into the air like a macabre hand mixer.

The smell of fuel stung my nostrils. *Fuel and smoke. Oh no!* I ran faster, pushing my new abilities to the limits. *"Liam! Gabriel!"* Masses of people surrounded the crash site.

For one deluded moment, I thought the mob of people were actually trying to help my mates. Then several figures lurched into the path of the spinning blade and were cut to pieces. More followed and met the same messy end.

I ducked as a bloody arm flew over my head.

They're zombies. I skidded to a stop. There had to be a hundred of those things. Every moment more dead fell out of a gaping hole in the skywalk and stumbled toward the heli-copter. Their shambling limbs made it impossible to get a clear view. *Please let my mates be okay.*

More and more zombies stumbled into the helicopter rotor and ended up splattered on the hotel wall. The snow around the aircraft quickly turned a deep rust color.

As disgusting as it was, I was thankful the spinning blade kept the dead at bay.

"Liam! Gabriel! Answer me!"

Liam met my telepathic shout with a groan. *"H-havana?"*

Relief made me dizzy. *"Liam! Are you hurt? Where is Gabriel?"*

"G-Gabe's not answering. I-I can't see... Too much smoke. The babes..."

"Liam!"

The smoke rising out of the rotor grew thicker as did the smell of gasoline. *"Liam, you have to get out of there!"*

The rotor made a grinding noise and stopped spinning.

My stomach dropped. *Oh, no!*

As if realizing the situation had shifted in their favor, the dead advanced on the helicopter. *I have to do something!* I threw back my head and howled.

None of the zombies even looked my way. *Shit!* Out of ideas and time, I barreled into the horde. My plan was to run straight through them, but I didn't count on them turning and reaching for me.

There were too many. A sea of dead crashed into me with snapping teeth and grasping hands. My fur and flesh ripped apart under their jagged fingernails. Battling through the excruciating pain, I kept running.

I have to save my mates! More dead piled on top of me. Teeth sank into my back and sides. Biting back my scream, I shook myself violently trying to toss them off. *Have to keep going.*

An eerie howl cut through the grating sound of their clicking teeth.

The zombies immediately backed away from me with the exception of one tenacious teenage zombie in a black ski jacket. He merely dug his teeth deeper into the back of my neck.

My breath came in an agonized gasp. I tossed my head from side to side trying to dislodge him.

A naked woman with silver eyes stalked toward us. She reached out and ripped the teenager from my back. She had a small build, but that didn't stop her from flinging the teenage zombie at the hotel wall with such force his head exploded like an overripe melon. Then she threw back her head and let out an eerie banshee-like cry.

She's like the guy who attacked Nathan. Shit. If Nathan couldn't take one of them down in a fight, do I even stand a chance?

The woman smiled. The sight of her bloodstained teeth chilled my blood. Over her shoulder I could see zombies tearing at the helicopter. The windows shattered under their fists. The cabin rocked back and forth.

Goddamn it. I didn't care what kind of monster the woman was. She was in my way. Growling, I launched myself at her.

With impossibly fast reflexes, she caught me by the throat and threw me down on the icy ground.

I thrashed in her grip, trying to claw and bite her. Every time I slashed her skin, it healed instantaneously. *Ah, hell.*

She let out an earsplitting shriek and crushed my throat in her fist.

Blood filled my mouth. Blinded by pain, I struggled to take a breath. My heart beat frantically. Knowing I had to shift, or I'd die, I forced my body to change.

Halfway through my shift, the creature snapped her jaws around my vulnerable human throat and began gulping my blood.

No! I tried to fight, but my limbs weakened and my thoughts grew sluggish. *She's too strong. Fuck! If I die my mates die.* Their handsome faces flashed in my mind.

Gabriel—my fierce, brooding warrior.

Liam—my gentle, protective giant.

Mason—my smart, sexy confidant.

Nathan—my...

My vision wavered. *I have to get free.* I beat against the woman's face and head.

She only drank deeper.

The sound of a little girl screaming rose above the roaring in my ears. *Mira! Mira is in the helicopter. She'll die in there.*

Anguished sorrow filled me. I shut my eyes and rallied my strength. *No. She will not die. I will not die.* I wrapped my hand around the woman's hair. "You'll die!" I wrenched the woman off my neck and kicked her away.

She landed on her feet in a catlike position. She lifted her head and let out a high-pitched shriek.

The sound triggered something predatory inside me. Without conscious thought, I began to shift. My limbs lengthened and my bones snapped as if I were changing into my wolf form. But as all my injuries healed, my muscles thickened and my frame continued to expand.

Instinct made me rock back on my hind legs. As I morphed into a strange form that was neither wolf nor human, a burst of incredible strength coursed through me. Throwing back my head, I let out a booming roar.

The woman, whose head now barely reached my hips, gnashed her teeth and came at me. This time, I caught her in one of my clawed hands and twisted her head off with the same effort Mira would use to pop the flower off a dandelion. Flinging her corpse away, I marched toward the helicopter.

Droves of zombies attacked, but this time their fingernails and teeth couldn't penetrate my thick hide. *Kick ass!* A swing of my massive arms sent them flying as if they were bowling pins. When they landed, I trampled over them until they were nothing but stains on the snow.

A flicker of orange flame near the helicopter rotor snared my attention. *Shit!* I raced over to the aircraft and ripped off the badly dented metal door. Smoke poured out.

Kneeling down, I peered inside. The first thing I saw was Mira.

Her silver-streaked hair glinted inside the smoky haze of the small space. She crouched on the floor clutching a doll.

I tried to say her name, but it came out a growl.

Mira let out a cry. "The Beast!" She tightened her arms around the doll.

With a start, I realized she was holding a baby.

The infant's head lolled back, its eyes open and unseeing.

My heart twisted. *Not everyone had survived the crash.*

Liam, still strapped into his seat, jerked up. The movement sent the blood dripping down his face onto the toddler slumped against the giant's chest. The toddler let out a cry.

Liam's eyes snapped open. He immediately bared his teeth.

"Liam, it's me."

His mouth dropped open. *"Havana? B-but how?"* His gaze widened as he scanned my monstrous form.

There was no time to explain. Not with smoke in the air and Gabriel slumped over the controls in the front seat. *"Can you walk?"*

Liam nodded and unbuckled his seat harness with a groan. His gaze went to the cockpit. "Gabe!" He reached between the seats and shook his friend's arm.

Although his chest rose and fell with labored breaths, Gabriel didn't move.

Liam gave me a worried look. "He looks trapped."

Crap. I let out a deep breath and tried to assure Liam. *"I'll get him as soon as you're out."*

Mira set down the infant's body and launched herself at me. "I won't let you hurt us!" Mira's tiny fist hit with as much impact as a butterfly wing. I hated that this form frightened her, but I needed its strength. I gently picked her up, ignoring her punches and kicks.

Cradling the crying toddler against his chest, Liam knelt down by the infant's body on the floor. My mate's face paled. "The babe is..." Liam couldn't finish his sentence.

It was heartbreaking, but there was no time to mourn. The helicopter could explode at any moment. *"We have to hurry!"*

Liam must've heard the panic in my telepathic shout. He scooped up the infant and stumbled toward me.

With my free hand, I pulled my mate out of the aircraft and pushed Mira at him. Thankfully, the little girl immediately quieted and wrapped her arms around Liam's leg.

"Head to the tram station." Mason could treat the surviving children for injuries.

Liam looked conflicted. His gaze went from me to the helicopter.

"Don't worry. I've got this." I hope.

My mate nodded and carried the children away.

Praying that the few zombie stragglers wouldn't be an issue for them, I leaned inside the helicopter. The rising heat scalded my face and the thickening smoke blinded me. Not a good sign. I had to get Gabriel out and fast. *But how?*

Several feet of snow entombed the front of the helicopter making it impossible for me to access it or the mangled door on the left side of the aircraft. Also, there was no way I could fit my hulking body between the two front seats.

The sense we were nearly out of time had me leaning in farther and wrapping my claws around Gabriel's seat. With a quick jerking motion, I tore out the entire seat with him still strapped in it. My stomach lurched when I saw the blood pouring from his mangled legs. *He'll heal,* I told myself as I cut through his seat harness with my claws, tossed the large male over my shoulder, and ran in the direction Liam had gone.

Three heartbeats later there was a loud explosion.

Oh shit! Needing to protect Gabriel, I dropped him onto the ground and fell over him. Heat scorched my fur. I ignored the fleeting pain and focused on covering Gabriel's body with mine. Something large and metal flew into my back. "Ugh." The pain from that was harder to ignore. Gritting my teeth, I hunkered down lower and held the position until I felt sure the worst had passed. Then I slowly pushed myself up and looked around.

Behind us, the helicopter lay in unrecognizable pieces. A few smoldering zombies shuffled around the charred wreckage. I turned to look in the direction of the tram terminal. There were several figures moving around in the snow.

"Mason, is everybody okay?"

"Havana! Bloody hell! Thank goodness you're alive." My bond with the doctor thrummed with relief and happiness. "Liam is taking out a few unwelcome friends that followed him over. Nathan is still unconscious, but the four children are just fine."

I must've not heard him right. *"Did you say four child—?"*

Mason interrupted me. *"Be careful. Liam says there is another super zombie out there."*

I snorted. *"I already took her out."*

"Really? That's brilliant. How's Gabriel?"

I looked down at my dark-haired mate. *"He's breathing, but his legs look like mush."*

"Is that all?" Mason made a relieved sound. *"He'll heal that when he shifts. What about you? Were you injured?"*

"No," I lied. The gnawing pain from the shrapnel in my

upper back was irritating the hell out of me. I tried to pull it out, but couldn't. *Fuck!* A snarl escaped my lips.

A pair of dark eyes snapped open and looked up at me.

"Gabriel!" Relief and joy made me dizzy. *"Mason, Gabriel is awake. Give us a minute and we'll come to you."*

Gabriel let out a choked sound.

I leaned down and tried to kiss him.

He jerked back at the sight of my huge, fanged jaw.

I couldn't blame him. If the situation were reversed, I probably would've peed myself. Giving him space, I moved back a few inches. *"It's me. Havana."*

He blinked hard. "P-princess?"

"In the flesh." I looked down at my claws. *"Or whatever?"*

He winced. "You've got a piece of the rotor sticking out of your back."

So that's what that was. I reached behind me again and used all my strength to yank the piece of metal out. The wound healed instantly. *Sweet!*

I inspected the long chunk of metal in my hand. In my human form, it would've instantly killed me. There were definite benefits to becoming a monster werewolf.

Gabriel tried to lift himself and let out an agonized gasp.

A hiss of sympathy escaped my lips. *"You have to shift, baby."*

With shaking hands he slid his jeans down. Then faster than I could blink, he shifted from human to wolf and back.

The sight of his healed legs eased the last of my anxiety. For the first time in hours, I could breathe easy. *Everything will be okay.*

Gabriel's strained expression disappeared and his complexion returned to a healthy bronze color. He stared up at me in awe.

Snow crunched behind us.

I whirled around to find a burning zombie shambling our way.

Gabriel jumped to his feet, but I'd already hurled the piece of rotor I'd been holding at it.

The flying metal sheered off the top of the zombie's head and embedded into the wall of the hotel with a loud *thunk*.

Gabriel gaped at the downed zombie and then at me.

"What?" Feeling self-conscious, I brushed off my furry thighs and rocked back to a standing position.

My fierce mate shook his head and did something I'd rarely seen him do—he laughed.

II

GABRIEL

I tried to find a comfortable position on the bench seat and failed. It, and the wood picnic tables that filled the top floor of the ski lodge, hadn't been build for a male my size.

Keeping my gaze on the doors that led into the large open eating room, I dug a splinter out of my elbow. It'd been hours since we'd finished our sweep of the ski lodge and the hotel next door, but we couldn't let our guard down. Especially now that we knew there were bigger threats than zombies out there.

The memory of that woman yanking the chopper out of the sky made me curl my hands into fists. That kind of strength was unprecedented among humans, or zombies or whatever she was. Although we'd destroyed every undead thing in the vicinity, the sooner we headed back to Sanctuary the better. Unfortunately, no one else seemed to feel the same urgency.

Over by the food service counter, Mason calmly tended the group of exhausted-looking human survivors. Most of them slept or lay dazed on the floor.

Havana, who'd shifted into human form and donned Liam's flannel shirt, also sat on the floor humming a lullaby. She reclined against the ledge of the large stone fireplace with the three children huddled around her.

Havana definitely had a way with kids. Even in sleep their small faces were turned up to hers. All in all, the babes didn't appear too scarred by their near-death experiences.

I, on the other hand, was still trying to choke down the fact that I would've died if Havana hadn't rescued me. It was humbling as hell to know I owed my life to my female. The female *I* swore to protect.

"We both owe her our lives," Liam corrected from the table on the opposite side of the room. *"Did you know Havana could do a hybrid shift?"*

I shook my head. *"Until now, I thought only the Originals could do that."*

"And until a week ago we thought Alphas were born, not made." Liam nodded toward our yellow-eyed mate.

I bristled at the reminder. Havana was defying everything we'd ever assumed to be fact about our species. It was unsettling. *"We need to talk to Mason."* Surely the doctor would have some insight into this new development. *"He's been with those humans long enough."* I started to stand.

"Patience, brother. They need medical care."

I huffed, glancing over at the ragtag group of humans. There wasn't one strong fighter among them. *"Why would Nathan stay and protect that pitiful bunch? He should have left them and gotten his daughter to Sanctuary."*

Liam adjusted the babe sleeping in his arms. *"Maybe he thought it was too risky to move Mira with those super zombies out there."*

I grunted, conceding his point. The fact that we hadn't found a single survivor in the hotel underscored how dangerous the situation had been. If Mira had been my daughter, I wouldn't have wanted to risk her life either.

I studied the little Alpha female curled in my mate's lap. She was a fey thing with her silver-streaked hair and her large golden eyes. Eyes like my infant niece. A phantom blade twisted my gut as I wondered what Isla would look like if she were still alive.

As if feeling my gaze, the little Alpha female opened her eyes and looked over at me.

I bowed my head in respect.

Mira ducked behind the long dark curtain of Havana's hair and shook the leg of the large male sprawled out next to them. "Daddy, the scary guy is looking at me."

"Let your daddy rest," Havana gently chided.

"Sorry," the little girl said looking crestfallen.

Havana patted Mira's back. "Don't worry, love bug. He'll be up soon. Go back to sleep."

He'll be up soon... A low growl escaped my lips. I'd be happy if Mira's father never woke. No matter how Havana had assured us she no longer had feelings for Nathan, I knew better. Before she'd learned how to block her thoughts from us, I'd shared her memories of Nathan and been shaken by the overwhelming love she'd had for the male. Even now she wanted him near and I'd caught her reaching out to touch him several times.

Fuck. What does that mean for us?

"It means nothing," Liam said, picking up my thoughts. *"Trust her. If she said he's in the past, believe it. Besides, she's claimed us. We're bonded for life."*

I snorted. *"Or until she breaks the bond."* Just as the Lykos female claimed her mate, she could unclaim him. It didn't happen often, but when it did it was devastating to the unclaimed males.

Liam frowned. *"She'll never do that. We're family."*

Since when had the deadly Enforcer become so naïve? *"You're deluding yourself. We've been together for all of a week. She's been in love with Nathan for much longer. Do you really think she'll choose us over him?"* My heart ached as I answered the question myself.

"Can you just for once stop being Mr. Doom and Gloom? Let's be thankful that we're here and we're all alive." Liam dropped his chin to plant a kiss on the wispy hair of the infant sleeping in his arms. Since discovering the babe hadn't died in the crash, Liam hadn't put her down.

Seeing the assassin turn into a ball of mush over an infant was as disconcerting as discovering my mate could take an all-powerful form. I shook my head wanting the world to go back to making sense.

The infant cooed and shifted in Liam's arms.

I studied the babe through narrowed eyes. Havana and Liam had been sure she'd perished in the crash, but the infant had roused minutes later. Mason concluded that the babe had only been knocked unconscious. Strangely enough, the doctor hadn't found a scratch on her. Her brothers had also emerged from their close brushes with death injury-free.

I turned my attention to the two boys sleeping near Mira and my mate. The resemblance of them to their mother was uncanny. I scowled. Their mother had nearly killed me today and their father had nearly taken out an Alpha male. That shouldn't be possible. No doubt, Havana would insist on bringing them, and all the other humans, back to Sanctuary. *Fuck.* I didn't like it. Not one bit. I scrubbed a hand over my face.

My mate's sweet scent enveloped me. I looked up to see Havana, standing next to my table. She laid her hand on my shoulder. "What's wrong, Gabriel?" Her presence eased my agitation and soothed me in a way nothing else ever had.

Forcing a smile I said, "I'm eager to get back."

"I am too." She slid in next to me on the bench. The warmth of her thigh felt welcoming against my leg. "At first light let's check the parking lot for vehicles that can make it up the mountain. There have to be some with tire chains. We'll all go up in a caravan."

Fuck. Just as I suspected she wanted to bring all the humans with us. "I don't—"

She interrupted me. "I know you don't like it, but you will have to deal with it, Gabriel. These people need our help. Once we get everyone settled at Sanctuary, I'm going to Sunridge. There may be other survivors in there and—"

I'd stop following the conversation as soon as she'd mentioned going to town. *No way.* I glanced out the closest window. "It's too dangerous. We don't know the situation over there. There could be hundreds more reanimated and—"

She raised her hand to cut me off. "That's why I'll be going there alone."

"Over my rotting corpse."

She crossed her arms over her chest. "Don't argue with me. I can become the monster werewolf—"

"It's called hybrid form," I corrected.

She rolled her eyes. "Whatever. Zombies don't bother me when I shift into...that thing."

Does she not understand her power? "In that form you're nearly indestructible." Realizing the truth of my words, my worry over her going into town faded.

"Nearly?" she said, rubbing the back of her shoulder.

"Your only real threats are decapitation, complete inciner-ation, and penetrating objects." It sounded like a lot, but when the hybrid could regenerate any other injury and were rumored to be immortal, it wasn't.

"That's a shame. I do so enjoy being penetrated." Her eyes glinted. She cast a quick look over at the sleeping children and slid her hand under the table to cup me.

My shaft hardened on contact. "What are you doing, princess?"

"Making sure you've recovered from your injuries." She slipped her fingers through one of the jagged tears in my jeans and brushed them against my stiffening flesh.

Lust blazed straight to my groin. I fought the urge to thrust against her hand. As much as I craved her touch, this wasn't the time or the place. "I've made a complete recovery."

"Have you?" She tightened her grip, making me groan.

I reached down to push her hand away, but somehow ended up folding my hand over hers.

She stroked my shaft from root to tip.

My eyes nearly crossed. *Fuck*. All thoughts of stopping her erotic play were replaced by the desire to haul her onto the table and mate her.

I must've been telegraphing my thoughts because Havana let out a husky laugh. "I don't think so, baby." Giving me a teasing smile, she pulled her hand away. "I think you're in fine health." She looked so fucking beautiful with her skin flushed, and her nipples pebbling against the fabric of Liam's shirt. The sweet scent of her desire fogged my brain.

"It's only right that I check on your health too." I clasped her thigh under the table and ran my hand under the hem of the flannel shirt.

Her beautiful ruby-red lips parted when I reached the apex of her thighs. She stiffened, but didn't object when I slid my fingers inside her.

I loved how hot and wet she was.

She let out a low moan and tried to trap my hand between her thighs. "W-we shouldn't. The children."

"They're sleeping like you said."

She licked her lips. "But the others." She glanced at Mason and Liam who were staring at us with hungry expressions on their face. It was obvious they sensed our rising passion.

Fuck them. This is my time. "Let's go somewhere private." Any of the empty rooms in the hotel would do. Hell, I'd mate her out in the snow as long as I got her all to myself.

"I-I don't know." Havana looked over at Nathan's sleeping body.

"I think you do." Pressing her thighs open with my palm, I found her clit and worked it until her eyes glazed over.

Her breath came in jagged pants. Her legs trembled, and I knew from the pleasure thrumming through our bond she was seconds from orgasming.

Not so fast. I yanked my hand away.

"Gabriel, please," she gasped, her fingernails digging into the wood bench.

It was time to reassert my sexual dominance. "Come with me, princess." I stood and offered her my hand.

She took it.

Excitement mounting, I all but dragged her out of the room. Before closing the doors behind us, I mentally called out to Liam, *"Keep watch while I'm gone. We'll be back soon."*

"Not too soon, I hope." His amusement came through our bond. *"Be sure to pleasure our mate."*

I looked down at Havana. *"Oh, I will."*

HAVANA

Anticipation wound through me as I followed Gabriel down the lodge stairs. I couldn't wait to get him alone and finish what we'd started.

Gabriel set a fast pace, and I struggled to keep up with him as he raced out the front door.

The cold night air was refreshing after being holed up in the top floor of the lodge. Even with the windows open, the smell of unwashed bodies made me nauseous. I really had no business complaining as I probably stank worse than anyone else. My hasty cleanup with some paper napkins and melted snow hadn't removed all the blood and zombie goo covering me.

Gabriel didn't seem to mind in the slightest. Sexual need wafted off my fierce warrior in waves. Giving me a wicked grin, he tightened his grip on my hand and pulled me toward the hotel entrance.

What a sight we would've been to any of the human survivors who might've glanced out the window—both Gabriel and I, barely clothed, walking barefoot across the snow. It was a good thing I'd compelled the survivors to be calm and ignore anything strange or unusual.

Although I felt guilty about using compulsion on them, it seemed justifiable. The calmer they were, the quicker Mason could treat them and the faster we could get to Sanctuary. I only wish I could similarly justify the compulsion I'd used on Nathan.

Unease swirled in my chest as I remembered how I'd forced Nathan to accept my claim. Just because I'd compelled him to save his life didn't change the fact I'd stolen his free will.

I let out a deep breath and watched it fog the icy night air. Even though Nathan had treated me like crap and broke my heart into a million pieces, he'd never mind-controlled me into being with him. I'd done that and more.

I'd bound him to me forever. No scratch that, I'd bound him to me and my three other mates forever. My palms began to sweat as I considered how they, and he, would react to that knowledge.

I looked up at Gabriel.

He clenched his darkly stubbled jaw as he steered me through the doors of the hotel. All evening he'd been worrying about Nathan.

Gabriel will lose his mind when he finds out what I've done. Inwardly cringing, I stumbled on the hotel carpet. Earlier, Liam had lit a fire in the large fireplace across from the hotel's front desk. The flickering flames seemed to be admonishing me. *I should have told Gabriel that I claimed Nathan.*

Gabriel stopped and looked back at me. "Is everything okay?"

No. I took a deep breath. "Yes." Spying a sign over his shoulder, I said, "Would you mind if we took a detour? I'd love a swim in the pool." It was a delay tactic and he seemed to sense it.

He arched one dark brow. "A swim?"

"To clean up a little." I motioned down at my body. I'd been tempted to take a dip in the pool earlier, but there hadn't been time.

Gabriel slowly nodded.

We changed direction and headed through the door near the elevators. It led straight into a long rectangular room. Although it was pitch-black in there, I could see the indoor lap pool surrounded by lounge chairs perfectly well. I could also see that in the far corner was a kidney-shaped Jacuzzi that looked large enough for a kindergarten class.

Trying to decide between the Jacuzzi and the pool, I inhaled deeply. The bleachy odor of chlorine brought back childhood memories of summers swimming in the pool at the trailer park.

"Come on," Gabriel yelled, diving into the pool.

I glimpsed his gorgeous ass before water splashed me in the face.

Laughing, I pulled off Liam's shirt and dropped it on top of Gabriel's discarded pants. Then I walked around to the other side of the pool and slowly descended the steps.

The wet caress of the icy water felt amazing against my bare skin. After wading in neck deep, I plunged underwater, submerging my face and hair. When I came up for air, I felt clean for the first time since yesterday's shower.

Something grabbed my thigh. I froze and looked across the pool at where I'd just seen Gabriel. *Oh, Jesus. Is there something in here with us?* My heart pounded as images of water-logged zombies filled my mind.

Gabriel surfaced next to me. "Boo!"

"Ah!" Giving him a dark look, I splashed water on his face. "Don't scare me like that."

He narrowed his gaze in challenge. "Or what?"

"Or I'll remind you who's in charge."

"Oh, really. And who is in charge?" Although his expression was teasing, there was an edge to his tone.

"Me," I replied, swimming closer to him.

"Are you sure about that?" He ducked into the water.

"Gabriel..." I backed up toward the shallower end of the pool trying to track his movements. Suddenly, I was scooped up and thrown into the air. I landed in the center of the pool with a loud splash. Spluttering, I surfaced. "Stop it!"

Gabriel swam up to me. "So who's in charge, princess?" he asked again in a silky voice.

"I—"

"Wrong answer." Gabriel picked me up and threw me into the deep end before I could finish my sentence.

Water filled my eyes and nose. I coughed and gave him a death glare. His behavior was ridiculous. "That's it. I'm never swimming with you again." My threat might've been more intimidating if I weren't treading in water with my feet unable to touch the bottom of the pool.

"I'll behave if you just admit that I'm in charge." His lips curled up in a half smile, but I could tell that there was more to this than him teasing me.

He's testing me. I didn't know much about wolves, but I knew they were always fighting to be top dog. Gabriel wanted to assert his dominance over me. *Fuck that.* In a flash, I shifted into the monster werewolf. My clawed feet hit the bottom of the pool as my furry chest rose far above the waterline.

Gabriel gaped up at me.

Being careful not to slice him to ribbons with my sharp claws, I picked him up and held him up over the water.

"Now who's in charge?" I brought him in for a close-up of my daggerlike fangs.

His eyes rounded before he averted his gaze. All the tension seeped from his body. His head bowed in submission. "You are."

"Right answer." My laugh came out as a monstrous roar as I tossed him into the center of the pool.

He landed with a splash so high, it nearly took out one of the lounge chairs.

Thrilled to have gotten the better of him, I shifted back into human form and swam to his side. "So are we done comparing dicks or whatever we're doing?"

"Yeah," Gabriel said, wading toward the pool steps.

"Hey." I reached for his arm, but he pulled away. Hurt pulsed through our bond.

In that moment, I realized I'd messed up big-time. Gabriel might be a Lykos, but he was also male. No guy enjoyed having his ego stomped all over. *Crap. How do I make this right?*

"I'll wait for you by the door," he said through clenched teeth.

Putting some speed into my kicks, I met him by the steps. "Don't go."

He spun around. "Why? It's clear you don't need me." He cleared his throat. "In the pool."

Ah. My fierce warrior thought I didn't need him. "But I do need you. In here," I pointed at my heart, "and in here." I grabbed his hand and pressed it against my core.

It seemed as if he would resist me, but then a flash of heat jettisoned through our bond. His gaze warmed, and he cupped his hand between my legs.

I let out a ragged moan as he parted my lips and slid a finger inside.

He found my G-spot with expert precision. "You do need me, don't you?"

"Yes," I gasped as he inserted a second finger. "You'll always be in charge when it comes to this." I grabbed his arm to steady myself.

He smiled as if I'd finally punched in the correct passcode. Then he worked his thumb over my clit. Once. Twice. The third time I came so hard, I lost my grip on him and slipped under the water.

Gabriel grabbed me before I could sink too far. In a lightning fast motion, he picked me up, set me on the top step of the pool, lifted my hips out of the water, and buried his face between my thighs.

Wow. The combination of the icy water and his molten hot mouth sent me into orbit. Whereas Liam went down on me with a hesitant sweetness and Mason with masterful expertise, Gabriel pleasured me with a ferocity that turned the act into something primal and all consuming. I screamed my throat raw as he devoured my pussy, licking, sucking, and stroking me into an endless chain of orgasms that blinded me with pleasure.

While I pleaded for rest, Gabriel sucked down my final orgasm with a satisfied smile. "There'll be no rest," he promised.

So blissed-out, I was barely aware of him turning me to face the pool ledge. I was half-in and half-out of the water on my hands and knees. The bump of his thick cock against my ass was all the warning I got before he kicked open my thighs and slid deeply into my core.

The erotic invasion had me seeing stars.

He didn't hold back, taking me harder and faster than he'd ever had. He gripped my hips and pistoned into me. His lust seared through our bond, inflaming my passion.

I rocked against him, demanding more, needing everything he could give me. My nipples scraped against the plaster step with each slam of his hips. *More. I need more.*

Water splashed around us, wetting the pool deck.

"Wider," he ordered, spreading my legs even farther with his muscular thighs.

I could only lean forward, bracing myself against the ledge of the pool.

His next thrust hit so deep, my eyes rolled back. "Oh, God!"

"Only I can give you this," he growled against my ear. "Only I can fuck you the way you need to be fucked, princess." There was a vicious desperation to his mating. He pinned me in place with his huge body, owning me, possessing me. Through our bond I could feel how much he needed me to submit to him, here and now.

"Yes, Gabriel," I cried, giving myself over to him. I tilted my neck to the side, exposing my throat. In this position, with his cock buried deep in my center and his teeth rasping against the side of my throat, I was completely at his mercy. Hybrid form or not, I was so vulnerable right now, he could end me.

He crooned his approval into my ear. Then he slid his hand between my legs and rubbed my clit.

I hurled over the edge of another orgasm.

With a roar of animalistic satisfaction, he slammed into me once more and came.

Quivering at the blast of wet heat filling me, I sagged back against Gabriel's chest. "Thank you," I gasped. That was exactly what I needed.

"Yes, thank you for the show," added Liam.

I jerked my head up and found the big guy standing with Mason by the door.

Liam strode over to the edge of the pool. "Can I get in on the action?"

"No!" Gabriel snarled.

"I could use a dip in there too," Mason added, his gaze on me not the water.

"Why are you dickwads here?" Gabriel groused, slipping out of my body.

Liam's sexy grin faded "Nathan woke. He's asking for Havana."

"His mate," Mason added quietly.

Oh, crap.

Gabriel scowled. "That's bullshit. Havana's not his mate."

Liam shrugged. "He's insistent she is."

Gabriel cursed. "Why the hell would he think that?"

My stomach sank to the bottom of the pool. I looked over at Mason.

The handsome doctor gave me a slight nod of encouragement. *"Best to get it out in the open, love."*

I swallowed hard and cleared my throat. "Because I claimed Nathan."

Liam and Gabriel stared at me with mirroring expressions of stunned horror on their handsome faces.

The moment of reckoning had come.

❦ 13 ❦

LIAM

I must've misheard Havana. She didn't just say she'd claimed Nathan, did she? As always, I looked to Gabe for answers.

Based on my friend's clenched jaw, he'd heard the same thing.

"I had to claim him." Havana licked her lips nervously, her gaze bouncing from my face to Gabe's. "If I hadn't, he would've died."

"And that would've been bad, why?"

Havana spun around to glare at Gabe. "He has a daughter."

"That we would've cared for," I said, softly. I planned to help look after all the babes we'd rescued, human and Lykos.

"Mira needs her father." Havana let out a sound of frustration. "You have to understand that claiming him was the *only* way to save his life."

Gabe grimaced. "If Nathan was as close to death as you say, you risked all our lives in claiming him."

"It was a calculated risk," Doc interjected.

Havana gave him a thankful look. "Mason thought I was strong enough to keep him alive."

Gabe shifted his gaze to Doc. "You encouraged her to claim the Alpha?"

The guilty look on Doc's face was damning.

Gabe took a step toward the doctor. "You gambled with our lives and then kept the truth from us?"

Motherfucker. A rumbling growl shook my chest. I glared down at the blond Omega.

Doc put his hands up and took a step back. "Don't come after me, mates. Havana begged me not to tell you."

"Because I was afraid of this reaction." Havana's gorgeous breasts swung from side to side as she stepped out of the pool.

As I tracked the water dripping down her mesmerizing curves, I suddenly found it hard to focus.

"Stop thinking with your cock, brother," Gabe mentally chided. *"She claimed Nathan just as I feared. Can't you feel his bond to her?"*

Shaking my head to clear my thoughts. I turned inward, probing the invisible connection that bound Gabe, Doc, and me to Havana. Among our bonds, there was a new link, thicker, and undeniably stronger. A knife blade of anxiety stabbed into me. "What does this mean for us?" I meant to send that thought to Gabe alone, but ended up blurting it out instead.

"Nothing. It means nothing," Havana answered in a soothing voice. "We'll just have one more plate at the table. Nothing has to change." She padded over to me and put her arms around my waist. Her nipples were stiff like berries and my attention turned to where they were pressing against my bare skin.

"The fuck it won't," Gabe shouted as he exploded out of the water. "You can't just add an Alpha male to our bond and expect nothing to change." His expression was thunderous, but I'd known him too long to mistake that look for anger.

He was scared. The greatest warrior I'd ever known was terrified he'd lose his female.

If he's worried, maybe I should be worried. My chest tightened as I looked down at our mate.

How could I compare to Nathan Steele? He was an Alpha male, the former Consort of the Alpha of Winterhaven, and her current ambassador. Before that, he'd been on the high council like his father before him. *I'm just Liam Murphy.* Forsaken by my mother who handed me over to Tasha when I was a child like an unwanted piece of furniture. Over the years, I'd worked hard to become the strongest and deadliest of the Winterhaven Enforcers, second only to Gabe. But I wasn't an Enforcer anymore. *I'm nothing.*

Havana tightened her arms around my waist. *"You're not nothing, you're my mate. And your name is Liam James now."*

Uneasiness kept me from returning her smile. Havana was the center of my world. Losing her would end me.

"Gabriel is correct," Doc interjected, a resigned look on his face. "Alpha males are the most territorial and possessive of our species."

He wasn't kidding. Alpha males allowed nothing to get between them and what they considered theirs. I stroked my hand over the smooth skin of Havana's back. "Nathan won't accept us, beautiful." *He won't accept me.*

Havana leaned back so she could look into my eyes. "Then I won't accept him."

My heart skipped a beat. "What?"

Gabe froze. "What are you saying?"

Havana twisted around to look at him. "I'm saying that I choose you over him. All three of you." She looked over at Doc. "I claimed Nathan to save his life, that's it. I have no interest in being with him. I belong with you." Pressing herself against me, she reached out her arms.

Doc took her right hand.

Although Gabe looked skeptical, he took her left hand.

Havana pulled the males so close we were all touching. "We belong together and nothing is—"

A feeling of overwhelming panic flooded my senses.

Havana's confused gaze swung across our faces. "What's that?"

Next to me, Gabe tensed. "It's him."

"Nathan must be worried about you," added Doc. Now that we were all bonded, Doc, like me, could sense Nathan's emotions.

Havana closed her eyes as if concentrating hard. "Damn. I can read his thoughts. He's freaking out thinking zombies got me." Havana dropped Doc's and Gabe's hands and stepped away from me. "I-I need to go back to the ski lodge and... explain things." She looked down at her naked body. "Crap. I need to find some clothes. I can't see Nathan like this."

"No, you can't," Gabe agreed.

Doc and I nodded. None of us liked the idea of him seeing her undressed.

She padded over to a pile of clothes on the ground and grabbed the shirt I'd loaned her. "I can't wear this either."

"Why not?" I enjoyed seeing her in my shirts. She looked sexy as fuck in them and it would send a clear message to the Alpha that she already had mates. Not that her smelling of chlorine and sex wouldn't do the same.

Havana whirled around to face me. "I smell like sex?"

"Uh, um, a little," I stammered. It always threw me when she read my mind like that. Normally, Lykos could keep their thoughts blocked from others if they wanted, but I was having a harder and harder time keeping Havana out of my head. Not that I wanted to. There was nothing I would keep from my mate.

"Not in a bad way," Doc added, trying to be helpful.

Gabe bared his teeth in his version of a smile. "You smell like you've been well fucked, princess."

Havana sniffed herself. "Crap! I do." She ran to the Jacuzzi and stepped in. Seconds later she was splashing water on herself and yelling, "Find me something to wear."

Gabe's expression darkened as she washed away all evidence of their encounter.

"Do you want me to check the hotel rooms to see if I can find something for you?" I'd kick down every damn door and ransack every room if it would please her.

"There's no time. Nathan is starting to lose his shit." Havana shut her eyes. By the way her brow furrowed I could tell she was concentrating hard. She snapped her eyes open. "I told Nathan not to worry, but he wants to see me right now."

"Of course he does," muttered Gabe under his breath.

"Could you wear this?" Doc pointed at a white terry cloth robe lying over one of the lounge chairs.

"That will work." Havana jumped out of the Jacuzzi, grabbed the robe, and pulled it on. "My hair must look ridiculous." She tried finger-combing her wet tangled locks. "God, what I wouldn't give for a hairbrush, a blow-dryer, and some product." Through our bond I sensed her agitation and a chaotic mix of emotions I couldn't quite pin down.

I'd never seen her flustered like this. Not even when the human ski instructor had stumbled on us mating in the cabin. I didn't know how to ease her stress, but I could at least help her with her hair. I pulled out the black comb I always kept in my back pocket and presented it to her. "Will this help?"

Her wide smile made me puff my chest out in pride. "Thank you, yes!" She immediately began raking it through her thick locks. "Ouch!"

"Not like that!" I took the comb back, stepped behind her, and gently ran it through her hair.

"Thank you, big guy," she said, leaning back against my chest.

Pleasure rippled through me. My sole purpose in life was keeping her safe and making her happy, if that meant combing her hair every day then so be it.

Gabe watched me detangle Havana's mane with a scowl. "Why do you care what Nathan thinks of your appearance?"

"Because the son of a bitch broke up with her," answered Doc, digging something out from under another lounge chair. "No one wants to confront their ex looking like rubbish." He lifted his head and looked at Havana. "Not that you could ever look like anything less than the goddess you are."

She blew him a kiss. "Thanks, hon. What are you doing under there?"

"Retrieving these." He held up a pair of purple flip-flops.

Havana let out a squeal. "Those are perfect!"

"Let's try them on, Cinderella." Doc strode over, knelt down, and helped slide her feet into them. He frowned. "They're too small."

"Not enough that it matters." Havana leaned down and kissed him on the top of his head.

A stab of jealousy pierced me. I wanted her to kiss me too.

Reading my mind, Havana turned, rose on her toes, and gave me a quick peck on my mouth.

I tried to deepen the kiss, but she pulled away with an apologetic smile.

"I need to deal with Nathan, sweetie."

I let out a sigh. "Yeah. I know." An irrational part of me hoped that if we ignored the Alpha, he'd go away.

The alarm bordering on hysteria pulsing through Nathan's bond told me that would not happen.

"We'll all go with you," Gabe announced, grabbing his mostly shredded jeans from the ground and yanking them on.

I nodded at him. *"Good idea. Maybe seeing the three of us with Havana will scare Nathan off."*

Gabe bared his teeth in a snarl. *"She's ours."*

Doc shook his head slowly. "I think it's better if Havana sees him privately."

Havana nodded. "I agree."

The fuck!

"No!" Gabe and I shouted at the same time.

Gabe stalked over to her. "There is no fucking way I'm letting you meet with him alone."

Refusing to be intimidated, Havana stared up at Gabe with her hands on her hips. "Let me? You can't be serious, Gabriel. No one tells me what to do, least of all the guy whose ass I just pulled out of a burning helicopter a few hours ago."

Gabe looked as if she'd just kneed him in the balls. As the Head Enforcer of Winterhaven, he'd been one of the most powerful Lykos in the faction for over a decade. No one, other than Tasha and Nathan, had ever put him in his place before.

I felt both sympathy for my friend's bruised ego and an even greater respect for Havana who was proving herself a powerful ruler in her own right. I cleared my throat. "I think Gabe's just concerned Nathan may use compulsion on you."

Havana's expression softened and some of her anger faded. "He won't."

"You don't know that." Gabe said, scrubbing a hand across the stubble on his chin. "He's one of the strongest Alpha males in the world. He's already compelled us—" he pointed at Doc and me. "What's stopping him from making you love him?"

Fuck. I hadn't considered that. To compel another Lykos to favor you was one of the basest acts possible. Even Tasha with her amoral behavior and psychopathic tendencies had outlawed it at Winterhaven. But we weren't at Winterhaven. None of the old rules applied.

Havana shook her head. "Nathan wouldn't do that, and even if he tried, he isn't able to use compulsion on me."

"But you don't know that for cer—"

Havana held up her hand to interrupt Gabe. "I do know this for certain because you said only a more powerful Lykos can compel another Lykos, and since I can turn into the monster werewolf, I'm more powerful than everyone."

"You're not more powerful than the Originals," Gabe corrected.

Tasha's menacing smile popped in my head. I shuddered. *Fuck Nathan. Tasha is the real threat to all of us.*

Havana waved her hand looking less than impressed. "Whatever. I'm not worried about them and I'm not worried about Nathan trying to mess with my head. I promise if he tries anything I'll just compel him to walk back to Saguaro Valley."

"That's a pretty thought, but no one can compel Ambassador Steele. No one," Gabe said, emphatically.

I nodded, thinking of the hundreds of times I'd witnessed Tasha try to compel Nathan. No matter how she wielded her power, the Beast had never gotten into the Alpha male's head. It might've gone easier for Nathan if she had for Tasha had resorted to torture and threats when compulsion failed.

"Not true." Havana chewed her lower lip. "I just compelled him a few hours ago."

Doc, who'd been strangely silent, piped up. "Havana is telling the truth. When she found Nathan he was near death, she compelled him to shift and he did."

Havana gave Doc a grateful smile.

Gabe looked as stunned as I felt.

I gave him a quick look over Havana's shoulder. *"Does this mean what I think it means?"*

"Havana is more powerful than the Beast," he murmured through our link. *"Fuck, she can challenge Tasha and if she does and wins, Havana can become our ruler."* His mounting excitement gave me pause.

"She's already our ruler," I said, reminding him of the oath we'd made to serve Havana and give up our old faction. *"And she's been an Alpha female for barely a week. You really want to put her up against a century-old killer?"*

Gabe paled. *"No. Fuck no. You're right. I got carried away for a moment. We need to keep her away from Tasha at all costs. But perhaps someday, Havana will be strong enough to take her on."*

"Someday." I agreed hoping that day never came.

"What are you two talking about?" Havana said, looking between Gabe and me.

Surprised she couldn't intercept our telepathic conversation, I pressed my lips against the top of her head. "We're just intrigued you could compel Nathan."

"Oh," she said looking down at her toes. "I feel terrible about doing it."

I tilted her face up and kissed her nose. "Don't feel bad at all. Nathan had it coming. Do you know he compelled the three of us to rescue you from the club the night we all met? Gabe didn't want to go."

Gabe shot me a dirty look. "Liam didn't either."

"I wanted to rescue you, love," Doc added, wagging his eyebrows.

"The hell you did, Mason," Gabe snarled.

Havana chuckled, but it sounded strained. "I'm not sure that's the same. I, um..." She looked down at her toes. "I didn't just compel Nathan to shift into a wolf. I also—"

"Vana!"

The war bellow would wake any zombies we hadn't obliterated.

"That's Nathan," Havana announced, stating the obvious.

"I better go deal with him. You guys stay here." She braced herself as if expecting another argument.

She wouldn't get one from me. "Yes, my Alpha." I bowed my head.

Gabe opened his mouth.

I gave him a hard look. *"Trust her judgment, brother."*

My friend pressed his lips together, looking none too happy. "Fine."

Doc nodded and the three of us watched her walk through the door.

As it snicked closed behind her, I hoped with every fiber of my being that nothing Nathan said would make her change her mind about him... or us.

❈ 14 ❈

HAVANA

Heart in my throat, I speed-walked through the lobby of the hotel. Each wet slap of my flip-flops on the red carpet seemed to rebound off the vaulted ceiling.

Emotions crashed through me with dizzying intensity. Worry, anger, excitement, guilt, and confusion, so much confusion. My feelings and thoughts tangled with Nathan's in an invisible twister-game leaving me unable to separate my emotions from his.

What I didn't reveal to my mates back at the pool was that my bond with Nathan was different from my bonds with them. Once my connection to the Alpha male had come online, it seemed to swallow me up whole. With the smallest bit of effort I could read every thought he had and feel everything he was experiencing.

Where is he now? I closed my eyes, and focused on our bond.

The freezing air seared his lungs as he stalked through

the snow to reach me. Anxiety choked him as he reached the doors to the hotel and flung them open.

Is Vana safe? Is she alone? Will she forgive me?

He spied me standing by the lobby desk. Relief pumped through his veins along with a feeling of love so intense it took my breath away. He strode across the lobby, his arms outstretched. "My little wolf!"

I OPENED MY EYES.

Nathan stopped a few feet away. He looked different. When I'd saved his life earlier, I hadn't had time to notice the gauntness of his cheeks or the salt-and-pepper beard he now wore. These changes in his appearance made him look wilder, more savage. "You *are* an Alpha. I-I thought I'd imagined that. How is that possible?"

His deep rumbling voice carried with it countless memories.

Nathan patiently reading Mira her favorite bedtime story every night.

Nathan telling Mira and me captivating tales of his international trips over our lunches.

Nathan singing softly to us both while we lay cuddled in his arms watching the flames in his giant fireplace.

Nathan professing his love as he thrust deep inside me hitting the spot that always made me unravel.

Nathan shouting at me that horrible night three months ago, *"You meant nothing to me."*

With the memory of those agonizing words ringing through my mind, I summoned a thick mental block between him and myself. As if I'd switched a radio off, I immediately stopped receiving his thoughts and feelings. Finally, able to take a deep breath, I answered his question, "It's a long story. How is Mira?"

"She's still sleeping with the other children." Nathan looked at me as if he was starved for the sight of my face. "I can't tell you how relieved I am to see you. When I woke, you weren't there. Liam and Mason said they would go get you, but they didn't return. I—" he thrust a hand through his untamed silver-streaked hair "—I thought something might've happened to you and—"

"And if I die you die," I finished for him.

"No. Yes. Fuck." Nathan's massive chest rose and fell with each breath. His beautiful golden gaze arrowed straight into my heart with the force of planets colliding. "I've missed you, Vana."

Ah, hell. He wasn't alone. How I'd missed seeing those beautiful eyes that could lighten to the color of sunlight or deepen to amber depending on his mood. And that's not all I missed. I dipped my gaze lower.

Since he wore only a blanket tied low around his waist, all his bronze skin was on display. He'd lost a significant amount of weight to where his ribs were stark against his smooth skin, but that didn't detract one iota from his attractiveness. In fact, the sharp lines of his cut pectoral muscles and defined six-pack abs made him even more swoon-worthy.

I couldn't help checking out his incredible V-shaped Adonis belt. He'd always loved it when I'd traced my tongue around it before taking him into my mouth. I grew damp as the memory heated my blood.

Nathan inhaled deeply. "You smell good."

He did too. Someone, probably Mason, had washed the blood from his body. There was only a faint trace of sandalwood in his rich masculine scent, but it was enough to awaken more memories. That woodsy scent had clung to his crisp white dress shirts that I used to enjoy undoing one button at a time. The silken sheets we'd cuddled on after a marathon of hot, toe-curling sex had also carried the scent.

My breathing came faster as I remember what an incredible lover he'd been. My nipples hardened against the fabric of the robe.

Nathan's eyes glinted. "I've been lost without you." He took another step forward.

The fierce chemistry that had always existed between us electrified the air.

A temporary burst of insanity made me want to cross the distance between us, hurl myself into his arms, and fuck all the hurt and anguish away. Instead, I locked my muscles in place. He'd shattered me when he'd tossed me to the curb like garbage. No matter how attracted I still was to him, I would not allow him into my heart again.

I took a shaky breath and schooled my face into a neutral expression. "We should talk." I motioned him toward a seating area near the fireplace.

Nathan blinked, seeming surprised by my icy tone. "Can we talk in the lodge? I don't like leaving Mira unprotected."

Even though I was angry with him, his concern for his daughter tugged at my heart. "I promise she and the others will be safe. We've killed every zombie within a mile of this place." I'd even double-checked every room of the hotel and lodge to be sure.

The tense expression didn't leave his face, but he followed me around the oversize Christmas tree to the cluster of armchairs.

I sat down slowly trying not to telegraph my own emotions. My thoughts were in a jumble and I stared into the flickering flames of the fire searching for the words I wanted to say.

Nathan sat in the armchair closest to mine. The brown leather barely contained his massive body. "I'm so glad you found me when you did."

"I am too," I answered honestly. No matter my conflicted feelings for him, I didn't want him to die.

"You fulfilled my greatest wish by claiming me." He reached out to take my hand.

I pulled away. "I feel bad I didn't give you a choice. But, I only did it to save your life. I want to end this—" I motioned between us "—union as soon as possible."

Nathan sucked in a breath. "You don't mean that."

I lied. "I do."

A look of devastation crossed Nathan's face. "Is this because of that misunderstanding three months ago? You're still mad about that?"

Misunderstanding? What the fuck? My carefully crafted statement went up in smoke. "Of course I'm still mad. You broke up with me in front of your fucking wife." Although Gabriel suspected Nathan had broken up with me to protect me from Tasha, he hadn't been there. He hadn't seen the coldness in Nathan's eyes that night.

A shadow darkened Nathan's face. "Tasha was never my wife."

"Okay." I waved my hand. "The mother of your child then. You even kissed her in front of me just before telling me I meant nothing to you." My voice grew tight.

A wave of pain hit me as the freshly healed wounds on my heart ripped open once again. I'd loved no one as much as I'd loved Nathan. He'd been my everything. My fairy-tale prince. My happy-ever-after. His betrayal had nearly destroyed me. If it hadn't been for Syd hiding the booze and kicking my ass out of bed, I don't know if I would've survived it.

Nathan pressed his lips together as if he were in pain. "I can explain everything."

I folded my arms over my chest. "Fine. Explain away." There wasn't anything he could say or do to redeem what he'd done, but I wanted to see him grovel.

"That night Tasha came to my home. If she'd discovered who you were, she would have gone on a rampage."

"Mmm-hmm." The wife coming home, what a clichéd scenario. I tapped my foot and looked over at the door to the pool. No doubt my mates were listening in with their super werewolf hearing, I should have brought Nathan somewhere else to talk.

Nathan cursed. "You're not even listening."

I swiveled around to glare at him. "Because it doesn't matter. You broke my heart, Nathan. You took our love, lit it on fire, and left me to wallow in the ashes."

"But—"

I held up my hand. "More than that, you broke my trust. Not only did you lie to me about Tasha, you kept things from me. Important things like the fact that I'm a freaking were-wolf and you are too. And why the hell didn't you try to fix this—" I put up my fingers in air quotes "—misunderstand-ing, before now."

"I was trying to protect you from Tasha. I'd planned to tell you before you transitioned."

I let out a laugh. "Well, you're too late, I've already transi-tioned in case you didn't get the memo. Also, I don't need protection from your ex."

He opened his mouth to say something, but I interrupted him. "Speaking of, did you fuck Tasha that night?"

"No!" he shouted emphatically. "I made sure she couldn't force me t—"

I raised my hand to cut him off. "Why should I believe you? You've already proven yourself a liar. I can't believe anything you say." I shook my head and said mostly to myself, "Why in the world would I want you as my mate?"

He fell to his knees in front of me. "Because I love you more than life itself. Because the only reason I broke up with you that night was to protect you from Tasha's wrath.

Because I'd planned on asking you to marry me that night." He held up a diamond ring.

The stone caught the light from the nearby flames and lit up like a prism.

Time seemed to stop. Choking on my breath, I looked from the ring to him and back. "Is this some kind of joke?"

He shook his head. "Remember that overnight trip to New York? It was to meet with a jeweler. I wanted only the best for my female." He laid the ring on my lap.

I picked it up with shaking hands. It was a gorgeous princess cut solitaire diamond, and it was huge. I'd eat my borrowed flip-flops if it wasn't at least four carats. "Nathan, this must've cost a fortune."

"There is no amount of money I wouldn't spend on you." The blanket around his waist started to unravel. He pulled the knot tighter and sat down on the armchair. "I had the night all planned. Le Ciel's was delivering your favorite—the beef bourguignonne along with that champagne you go wild for. I was going to propose after dinner."

"You were?" The floor seemed to sink under my chair. Never in a million years did I imagine Nathan planned on proposing. Hell, every time I'd brought up moving in together, he'd changed the subject. I'd figured he was commitment phobic or ashamed of me.

"Yes, but when I got home, I found Tasha and her Enforcers inside. She'd tortured and killed the delivery guys along with Rachel."

Oh no! Not Rachel! I'd adored the sweet, deaf older woman. She'd been a welcome replacement for Nathan's stuffy prior housekeeper.

Nathan pressed his lips together in a grim line. "Tasha butchered her like a piece of meat."

Tears filled my eyes, but my grief gave rise to anger. "I'll kill that bitch."

Nathan shook his head. "This is why I didn't tell you about Tasha. I knew this is how you'd react and I had to protect you."

This time when Nathan reached out to take my hand, I let him.

"That night, you rang the doorbell at the worst possible time. I knew if Tasha found out who you were, she would have made what happen to Rachel look merciful."

I narrowed my eyes. "I'd like to see her try."

Nathan tightened his fingers around mine. "You don't understand. Tasha's a sadist. Her only joy is inflicting pain on others. I should know." His eyes clouded over with the kind of desperate sorrow I'd only seen in abuse survivors.

Jagged puzzle pieces started coming together. Nathan's strange moods. His fixation with BDSM. How over the top protective he was of Mira. "And she inflicted pain on you?"

"Yes," he answered in a clipped voice, his strong jaw ticking with emotion. He pulled his hand away and turned to stare at the flames.

As silence grew between us, I realized he wouldn't reveal any other details. *Screw that.* He'd kept the truth from me our entire relationship, I wasn't going to let him hide anymore. I tucked Nathan's ring into the front pocket of my robe and closed my eyes. Focusing my attention inward, I tore down the mental blocks I'd put between us. A torrent of Nathan's anguished memories came at me.

Tasha bringing her whip down, over and over on Nathan's small back as he tearfully begged her to stop. Her maniacal laughter burning in his ears as she beat him until he passed out.

Tasha forcing him to watch her boil, draw and quarter, dismember, and skin her enemies until they begged for death.

Tasha cutting off his clothes, shackling him to her bed, and abusing him.

I sucked in a breath. *He'd been a child.*

Another memory flew at me.

Tasha threatening a now grown Nathan to do her bidding. Him refusing and later seeing the head of a close friend mounted on Tasha's trophy wall.

Tasha holding a knife over a small newborn baby. Nathan making a desperate bargain to protect the infant—

"Mira." I gasped and opened my eyes. "You wore the silver cuffs to protect Mira." Only now did I understand the silver had prevented him from shape-shifting, healing, or having sex.

Nathan jerked his head around to stare at me. "You read my mind?"

"I needed to know why you feared her. Oh, Nathan. I'm so sorry." I reached out and wrapped my arms around him. He'd endured so much at her hands. So damn much. "I had no idea."

"I never wanted you to know." His shame pulsed through our bond.

I pulled away and stared into his eyes. "Don't you ever be ashamed of what that psychopath did to you. You are an incredible person." I meant every word. It amazed me he could come from such a tormented childhood and still become such a caring father. Yes, he was moody as hell. Yes, he'd kept things, very important things, from me. Yes, he'd broken up with me, but I could see now that he'd done it out of love. *How can I hate him for that?*

His eyes glinted with emotion. "That's why I love you so much. Even after seeing all the pain and darkness, you still think I'm a worthy male."

"Because you are. Hell, Nathan. I don't know any guy who'd give up sex indefinitely for any reason." He'd been willing to do anything to save his daughter. I would have fallen back in love with him for that alone.

His lips quirked up. "I'd never been tempted to break the oath I made to Tasha, until a certain beautiful female in a tight skirt waltzed into my office for an interview."

"Oh, yeah," I said, returning his smile. A smoldering heat flickered between my thighs. The indefinable electrical charge between us hummed to life, bringing with it an aching sexual hunger. For him.

"Continuing that interview was one of the toughest things I've done. All I wanted to do was set you on my desk and bury myself inside you." His voice was rough and low.

My breath grew choppy at the memory of our first encounter. "All I wanted to do was mount you on your office chair."

Nathan let out a groan. "Please tell me you forgive me, Vana. I love you so much."

His words rang with truth.

Something inside my chest broke open and released all the anger and bitterness inside. No matter how I'd tried to deny it, I was still in love with him and I always would be. However, I didn't want him to think he could win me over so quickly. "Fine. I forgive you. But you have a lot of groveling to do. A lot."

"I'll be your personal slave for the rest of your life, if that is what you want."

I smiled at the image of him waiting on me hand and foot. "As tempting as that is, what I need right now is your promise never to lie to me and never to keep anything from me."

"I swear on my life." He brushed his mouth over my knuckles. The sensation of his lips on my skin sent a shock wave of need crashing through me.

A moan escaped my lips.

His hungry gaze met mine and a surge of desire flooded our bond. I didn't know if the lust I felt was his, or mine. Frankly, I didn't care.

I leaned over the chair. "Kiss me."

He let out a low growl. Then in one fluid movement picked me up and dragged me into his lap. His mouth claimed mine. Our lips and tongues danced as our hands tore at the fabric barriers between us. He pulled open my robe at the same time I unknotted his blanket.

A hiss escaped my lips as he latched on to my nipple and suckled. Arching against his mouth, I reached down and took his thick hard cock in my hand. I couldn't wait to have him inside me again.

❧ *15* ❧

NATHAN

raise the fates. My daughter and I had survived insurmountable odds and my female had forgiven me.

Vana slid her hand back and forth on my cock, mastering me with her soft touch. Each stroke drove me more insane with lust.

I fought the urge to throw my head back and howl. Instead, I thrust wildly against her palm, all my reputed self-control going up in flames.

As I lost focus, Vana's nipple fell out of my mouth with a small pop. I wanted to lick and suck that dusky peak the way she liked, but I was held captive by her measured strokes. My balls tightened to the point of pain. I needed to be inside her. *It's been too fucking long.*

"Only three months," she said, with a teasing smile.

It should've been shocking she could read my thoughts so easily. Not even Tasha could breach my mental blocks. But Vana and I were bonded now, and a lifetime of sharing my mind with my best friend Ty had made it second nature to open myself up to someone I loved. And I love Vana above all others. "Those three months were an eternity."

Her eyes glowed in the firelight. "Then we should take our time." Her strokes became tortuously slow.

Damnation. I didn't know if I could take this much longer.

She froze as if remembering something. "We need to talk about the others."

"You said Mira and the humans would be safe next door." After we'd mated we'd go check on them. I drew Vana's nipple back into my mouth.

"I don't mean the survivors—ah..." she broke off as I suckled hard. "I-I can't think when you do that."

I inhaled deeply, drawing in her scent. Chlorine had muted her exotic floral scent, but it couldn't overpower the sweet musk of her growing desire. *She wants me.* That knowledge burned through me like a blowtorch and triggered my inner wolf. Raw, primal need clawed to the surface.

Fuck going slow. I shifted her thighs open wider.

She stiffened and braced her hands on my shoulders. "Nathan, I have something very important I need to—"

Lust rode me so hard, I couldn't pay attention to her words. I couldn't pay attention to anything but her core poised an inch from my throbbing dick. The need to be inside her ravaged my mind. All it took was a rock of my hips and I was buried inside.

Her golden eyes rolled back. "Oh, Nathan," she moaned. She flattened one hand against my chest, grasped the arm of the chair with her other hand, and rolled her hips. She was hotter and wetter than she'd ever been before.

I gasped. "Yes, my little wolf, take all of me." Why hadn't we ever fucked with her on top before? It was mind-blowing.

She rocked up and down, teasing me with achingly slow pumps. She didn't understand how close I was to losing control.

"Vana," I pleaded.

She looked down at me, her eyes heavy with passion. "What?"

"Next time we'll take our time," I promised. All the while we'd dated, I'd kept a tight rein on the raging beast inside me, only allowing her to see small glimpses. Now that she'd transitioned, I didn't need to worry about hurting her. I could unleash it all.

Gripping her hips, I lifted and dropped her on my cock with such speed and intensity that her head snapped back. As I brought her down over and over, I punched my hips, driving deep into her.

"Nathan!" she cried in delight, writhing against me. Incredibly she moved with me, taking it all and demanding more.

My incredible female. I captured her mouth and matched the thrust of my tongue to the wild tempo of our coupling.

Her nails scored down the sides of my shoulders, drawing blood as I pounded into her.

I couldn't have cared less. Merciless lust drove me to mate her as hard and fast as I could. I'd missed this so much. The music of her moans. The feeling of our slick skin rubbing together. The viselike grip of her pussy around my cock.

The animalistic sounds of our pleasure filled the room.

She trembled over me, her thighs quivering around mine. From experience, I knew she was close to climaxing. How I wanted to tie her down and draw out her orgasm. Make her beg for it. But raw, primal need had taken over.

"Yes!" She ground against me, chasing sweet release.

Needing to give it to her, I slipped my hand between our bodies and stimulated her clit.

She came apart. "Yes. Oh, God! Nathan!"

As she screamed her orgasm, I couldn't hold on anymore. I pumped into her once, twice, and then came so hard my vision flickered.

Breath sawing in and out, she collapsed on top of me.

I crushed her against my chest, my cock still pulsing inside her. I didn't want to break the connection between us. Ever. "I love you," I panted.

"I love you too," she gasped.

Thank the fates. The enormous weight I'd been carrying for months evaporated into the air. Since the night Tasha forced me to deny my female I'd felt only half-alive. With Vana in my arms, all was right in the world. After we'd mated at least three more times and I'd properly restaked my claim on her body, we'd go next door and get Mira. Then we'd head to Sanctuary with the humans and plan the next step in our lives, together. Nothing would impede our happiness. Nothing. Not the apocalypse. Not Tasha. Not—

The sound of heavy footsteps brought my head around.

Three males stood in the middle of the lobby staring at us.

I immediately recognized Mason and Liam, but it took me a second to place the scowling dark-haired male. Gabriel, Tasha's favorite Enforcer, looked different without his eye patch.

Although rationally I knew the males had helped to save our lives, I couldn't stop the instinct to snarl at them. Having three unclaimed males that close to my naked female wasn't acceptable. I swung Vana off my lap and jumped in front of her protectively. "Give us a moment, please."

The males ignored me.

"What the fuck, princess? You said you were going to unclaim him."

Vana stepped away from me, her eyes darting furtively around the lobby. "I was. I-it's more complicated than I thought."

Liam crossed his arms over his gargantuan chest.

"Doesn't look that complicated to me. You mated him." He turned to look at Mason. "You were right, Doc. You win the bet."

The doctor gave the redheaded giant a smug grin that faded as he stared at Gabriel's thunderous expression. "Gabriel, take a deep breath. You need to relax, mate."

Why the fuck did Gabriel care that we mated?

Tasha's Head Enforcer clenched his jaw so tight it popped. "Relax? How can I relax when our Alpha is fucking him?"

Gabriel's words confused me. *Tasha is his sworn Alpha, right?*

"It's her choice, mate." Mason looked over at Vana, a forlorn expression on his face. "You know how I feel about you. It will hurt like bloody hell to let you go, but your happiness matters more than anything."

Let her go? I inhaled again, picking up something I'd missed before. These males weren't unclaimed. They carried the scent of my mate in their blood. They were hers. All. Fucking. Three. Of. Them.

A knee-jerk kick of denial hit me in the gut. *No. No fucking way.*

I spun around to confront Vana.

The pained look on her face told me all I needed to know. *Fuck the fates.* "You claimed these males."

"I-I tried to tell you before..." she trailed off.

Pain lanced through my chest, wounding me deeper than any torture Tasha had ever devised. *How did this happen?* Vana was mine. Mine alone. Ty had assured me she hadn't so much as been on a date with anyone else these past three months. *How could everything change in ten days?*

"Why?" I had to ask her. *Why didn't she wait for me? Why wasn't I enough for her?*

She chewed her lips. Lips that just minutes ago had been

fused to mine. Lips that the other three males had no doubt tasted.

An inferno of rage erupted inside me. "You betrayed me."

Vana lifted her chin, her eyes sparking with anger. "I did no such thing. You broke up with me."

"I know, little wolf." My words were not for her. As painful as it was to admit, I couldn't fault my female for taking a lover. Not when I'd made her think I didn't care. But I sure as shit could blame the dark-haired bastard I'd entrusted with her care.

I swung my gaze to Gabriel and growled at him. "I warned you what I'd do to any male that touched her."

The motherfucker had the nerve to stand his ground. "She claimed me, Nathan. I am hers."

"I am hers," murmured Liam.

"I am hers," echoed Mason.

Their words triggered the territorial beast inside me. "No!" The calm veneer I'd worked so hard to adopt as the Winterhaven ambassador sheered away leaving only the snarling wolf behind. "She's mine!" I let out a roar so loud the ornaments on the Christmas tree shook.

Liam dropped his gaze.

Mason lowered his head in submission.

Gabriel glowered back. "We belong to her."

The Beta dared to challenge me? Rage pumped through my veins. My vision tunneled.

Vana said something. I couldn't hear her over the popping of my joints and bones. As soon as my paws hit the floor, I charged Gabriel.

The Enforcer yanked off his pants, shifted into a wolf, and met me halfway. We ripped into each other with snarling teeth and razor-sharp claws.

Blood spewed.

Fur flew.

We were closely matched in size and had trained together as boys, but I'd spent too much time inside boardrooms while Gabriel had been honing his fighting techniques. It was all too clear the other male had the upper hand when he pinned me down and tore a sizable chuck out of my hide.

Fuck. That hurt.

"Stop!" screamed Vana.

Liam locked his arms around her to keep her from getting between Gabriel and me.

"Stop it, right now!" Vana cried, struggling against Liam's hold.

Gabriel turned his head to look at her, giving me the opening I needed.

I lunged for his throat.

Sensing my attack, Gabriel shifted into human form. His sudden increase in size threw off my strike.

I shifted too and pounced on the male.

Then it was a flurry of punching and kicking.

Damn the fates. Gabriel was good.

While I was unleashing every ounce of my fury on him, I got the sense he was holding back. That infuriated me even more. I let out a roar.

He responded with a nasty uppercut to my jaw. *Fuck!* I spat out a mouthful of blood, grabbed Gabriel by the shoulders, and slammed him into the lobby counter.

Papers scattered and a small silver call-bell crashed to the floor with a loud *ting*.

Vana had somehow gotten free from Liam. "Gabriel! Nathan! Stop it right now!"

There's no stopping this. I gnashed my teeth and planted my fist into Gabriel's stomach.

He let out a gratifying *oumpf*.

Before I could savor the hit, he roundhouse kicked me in the chest and sent me careening straight into the Christmas tree. The nearly twenty-foot Douglas fir and all the ornaments smashed to the ground.

Gabriel stalked over while I was trying to untangle myself from a string of Christmas lights. "Stay down if you know what's good for you." He raised his fist over my head.

I never played dirty, but this wasn't a fight I could afford to lose. "Knock yourself out," I shouted with a heavy dose of Alpha power.

Gabriel froze. An expression of helpless rage crossed his face. He shook his head trying to fight the compulsion, but there was no way he'd succeed.

At the end of the day, I was an Alpha and he was a Beta. Our position in the Lykos hierarchy had been established at birth and, no matter how skilled a fighter he was, I would always dominate him.

With a frustrated growl, he punched himself repeatedly in the face.

"Hey! No fair using powers," shouted Liam.

"Enough!" Vana's voice held more power than any Alpha I'd ever encountered.

Stunned into silence, I could only watch as she strode over to Gabriel. "Disregard Nathan's command."

Gabriel stopped hitting himself and gave me a disgusted look. "Resorting to compulsion makes you look weak, Alpha Steele."

"I don't care what you think, Enforcer Perez," I spat.

"I'm Gabriel James now," he replied, looking over at Vana.

Vana stopped in front of me, looking like an avenging angel with her hands on her hips and her eyes spitting fire. "Nathan, you will never under any circumstances use compulsion on my mates. Do you understand me?"

Her shout reverberated in my suddenly aching head. *So this is what it's like to be compelled?* Never before had any other Lykos been able to mind-control me. I'd thought she'd only been able to compel me earlier because I'd been near death. Obviously it hadn't been a fluke. Helpless to resist her power, I nodded.

"I need to hear you say it," Vana demanded.

I gritted my teeth. "I swear to never use compulsion on your mates." *Damn the fates.* This isn't at all how I hoped our reunion would go.

Mason walked over. He swept a clinical gaze over my body. "You have several contusions. You should shift and heal them."

"I'm fine." I glared at the blond Omega. I'd never considered Tasha's doctor a threat, but knowing he'd mated my female made me want to snap his neck.

Avoiding Mason's outstretched hand, I stood. The bruises on my face and torso throbbed, but I'd be damned if I showed these males they bothered me.

As I approach Vana, Gabriel and Liam moved in—forming a protective Lykos shield around her.

Aggravation made me fist my hands. "Move out of the way."

Liam called out, "We don't want to fight with you, Nathan."

I snarled. "Then you shouldn't have taken what was mine."

Gabriel snarled back. "We're hers, accept it or—"

Vana let out a shrill whistle. "Guys, go back over to the lodge and check on the survivors. Nathan and I need to talk. Alone."

Gabriel gave her a disgusted look. "We all saw how well that turned out last time."

"Now, Gabriel!" her voice boomed.

"Fine," he snapped. Gabriel stepped forward, so we were eye to eye again. "I'm looking forward to a rematch. The next time I won't hold back."

The need to assert my dominance had me snarling, "I'll break you in half."

"Doubtful." Gabriel sneered.

Vana huffed. "I swear to God if you two fight again, I will compel you to be best friends."

She wouldn't?

Gabriel and I exchanged an uneasy look before he and the other two males headed for the door. Once there, Gabriel looked back at me. "We're hers, Alpha Steele. Deal with it."

"Oh, I'll deal with it all right." Whatever bond Vana had formed with these assholes would be undone as soon as possible.

16

HAVANA

I bit back a relieved sigh when Gabriel stepped out the door. The crackling tension in the room dissipated and Nathan relaxed his aggressive posture.

For a minute I'd worried the two of them might actually kill each other. I hadn't expected that reaction from Mr. Cool, Calm, and Collected, but maybe I should have. Clearly, I didn't know Nathan as well as I thought I did. I leaned back against the front desk and studied him.

Nathan stared at the front door, his chest rising and falling rapidly. "I'm sorry you had to see that. I usually side with diplomacy over fists, but Gabriel betrayed my trust."

"Like you betrayed mine?"

Nathan twisted his head around so fast he might've gotten whiplash. "I thought we'd cleared everything up." He motioned at the armchairs by the fireplace.

I put my hands on my hip. "I may have forgiven you, but that doesn't mean I'll ever forget what you put me through." Those emotional scars would last a lifetime. Pain balled inside me as I dragged in a deep breath. "Do you know when I was a child I used to dance around my tiny room in the trailer imagining the prince who'd rescue me from my lonely life?"

Nathan blinked. "Uh, no."

"The sad thing is, even when I grew up I never stopped believing it. Ridiculous, I know." My fairy-tale castle had become Nathan's palatial estate in the foothills and our horse-drawn carriages had become his fancy sports cars.

Nathan shook his head and stepped closer. "It's not ridiculous. I too longed to find my mate. I longed to find you."

It hurt to hold his heavy stare, but I did anyway. "I thought you were my prince, Nathan. My happy-ever-after. But then you hurt me more than anyone else ever has." I rubbed the area over my heart. "Because of that, I no longer believe in fairy tales. But I do still believe in finding whatever happiness you can. Liam, Mason, and Gabriel make me happy."

"I can make you happy." He thrust a hand through his hair. "I'm sorry for robbing you of your romantic notions. I'm sorry for how badly I handled things three months ago. And most of all I'm sorry for forcing those males on you."

Although his expression didn't change, jealousy and self-blame blasted through our bond. A muscle ticked below his eye. "This is all my fault. If I hadn't compelled those fuckers to bring you to Sanctuary, you wouldn't have mated with them."

"True, but then I would be dead," I replied, tightening my robe belt.

Nathan's brows rose. "What?"

"Liam saved me from a group of zombies that night." I shuddered thinking of my close call in the club alley. "And later, when I'd found out I'd been infected, Mason cured me." I left out the part where the doctor also saved me from freezing to death. There was no need to discuss my dumbass decision to walk up the side of the mountain during a winter storm in heels.

"You were infected with the Z-virus?" Nathan's voice rose a notch.

"Unfortunately." I rubbed the palm of my hand feeling for the phantom evidence of the cut that nearly ended my life. "Thankfully, Mason used some unorthodox methods to speed up my transition to a full Lykos." Anticipating Nathan's next question, I added, "It involved a transfusion of Tasha's blood that gave me her superpowers or whatever." I pointed at my yellow eyes.

Nathan blinked hard. "I'd wondered how you transitioned into an Alpha. I'd assumed it was because your fa..." He broke off and cleared his throat. "I think I understand now. You claimed Liam, Mason, and Gabriel out of appreciation, because they saved your life."

He didn't understand a thing. I gave him the unvarnished truth. "No. I claimed them because they were there for me when I needed them, because I wanted a family, and because I want to fuck their brains out for the rest of our lives."

He flinched, but I didn't take back my words. If this was going to work we had to start being honest with each other.

"You don't need them." Nathan crossed the distance between us. "I swear from now on, I will always be there for you. Mira and I will always be your family. And you can fuck me brainless for eternity." He reached out and dragged me into his arms. "I want to go to bed inside you every night and wake up beside you every morning. I want us to raise Mira together and, if the fates bless us, have more young together. We will make the big family you always wanted."

I smiled into his broad chest. "That sounds nice. But my other mates will be part of the family too."

He pulled away, the glow in his eyes fading. "I won't share you with those fuckers."

I sucked in a breath. "Even if that means losing me?"

An expression of pain crossed his face. "You'd choose them over me and Mira?"

A tight knot formed in my chest. "There doesn't have to be an either-or."

"Damn the fates, Vana. We love each other. I was getting ready to propose to you." He motioned to the pocket of my robe where I'd stashed his ring. "You don't even know these other males and if you did, you'd be sickened by the atrocities they've committed. All three of them were loyal servants to Tasha."

"As were you, Ambassador Steele." Funny how when we were dating I'd always suspected Nathan was in the mafia. Turns out his real job had been even shadier.

I took a deep breath. "I know you don't like this situation, but I need you to accept it. I love you, but I care about Liam, Gabriel, and Mason too. I'd like us all to be together." In my mind's eye I pictured us all gathered in one of Sanctuary's huge living rooms. Mira was playing with her redheaded, blond, and dark-haired half siblings. There would be laughter and love enough to fill that colossal house.

Nathan lowered his brow and wrinkled his nose. "No, absolutely not."

The finality of his tone ripped my dream to shreds. "Could we at least try it?"

"Fuck, no."

So much for that idea. *Gabriel is right. Nathan will never accept my other mates.* I stepped away from Nathan, my eyes stinging.

He reached out and grabbed my arm, stopping me from walking away. "Vana please don't cry. Look at it from my point of view. What if I propositioned you with the reverse situation? What if I was standing here asking you to share me with three other females I just met?"

My claws and teeth lengthened at the very idea of another woman touching him.

"Do you see my point, little wolf?"

Unfortunately, I did. But it didn't change the fact that I'd claimed Liam, Mason, and Gabriel. Despite not knowing them long, my ties with them went soul-deep. It was impossible to describe the connection. The closest thing I could compare it to was when I'd seen a friend of mine give birth. The moment Donna had held my godchild, Gavin, in her arms there had been an instant, incredible bond there. A romantic version of that imprinting had formed between my mates and me and to even consider severing that link made it hard to breathe. "When I claimed them, it was for life."

"When you claimed them, you thought I didn't love you." He let out a pained laugh. "The word love doesn't even cover it. I adore everything about you. Your courage. Your tender heart. Your amazing way with children. Your sharp mind. Your openness to new experiences in and out of the bedroom. The way you dance. The way you tell stories, waving your hands up in the air." He waved his hands in front of his face.

I gasped. "I don't do that."

"You absolutely do that and I love it. I even love your snoring."

"What? I don't snore."

He chuckled. "You do. Like a hibernating bear, but I still find you the sexiest damn thing on this planet." He wove our fingers together. "Apparently, in my family we know right away when we've found our chosen." His eyes got a faraway look. "We only love once and we love forever." He looked down at me. "You are my chosen, Vana."

My stomach flipped. I loved him too. So, so much.

"Choose me, Vana. Choose me and Mira who needs you almost as much as I do."

My heart ached at the mention of the little girl. *If Nathan and I separated, will I ever see her again?* I rubbed my chest, feeling as if I was being ripped apart. "Nathan, I—"

He held his hand out to cup my face. "I know what I'm asking isn't easy and it isn't fair after what I put you through, but I swear if you choose me, I'll spend the rest of my life making it up to you."

"And if I don't choose you," I whispered.

Sadness clouded his eyes. "Then I'll go through life missing the other half of my soul. I hope to the fates that isn't your choice."

My throat clogged. "I-I don't know. Nathan, this will tear me apart."

"I'm sorry for that, little wolf. I wish I could go back and do a lot of things differently, but then again it still might've led us to this moment. Make a choice—Mira and me or them." He motioned at the door.

I shook my head, not wanting to choose.

He cleared his throat. "You should know once you've broken a bond with a mate, it can never be remade."

Great. So not only was this decision going to be heart-wrenching, there were no do-overs. "I-I'll need some time to think."

A look of disappointment settled on his rugged face. "Fair enough. I'll go see if Mira's awake." He gently dropped my hand and stepped away. Although I'd asked him to leave, tears welled in my eyes as I watched him walk over to the armchairs, grab his blanket, knot it around his waist, and walk to the door.

He paused in the entryway. "I love you, little wolf."

"I love you too, Nathan," I whispered.

He gifted me with one of his heart-stopping smiles, and then he was gone.

Ah, hell. What am I going to do?

17

MASON

Havana's mind brushed against mine like a soft caress. *"Mason, can we talk?"*

I froze amid scavenging the shop at the ski lodge. The half convenience store and half ski rental had turned up a surprising array of medical supplies. Searching it had helped occupy my mind and kept me from worrying about Havana. Or more specifically, worrying about losing Havana. *"Of course. Did you want me to go back to the hotel?"*

"Please." A wave of sadness pulsed through our bond.

I groaned. Not only did it flay me to know my mate was in distress, but my intuition told me she would not be my mate for much longer.

Bollocks. I looked down at the box of crushed Band-Aids in my fist. I wasn't a consummate pessimist like Gabriel, but from the moment I'd caught Havana's sheer panic over Nathan's fate back at Sanctuary, I'd seen the writing on the wall.

No matter how he'd hurt her, she loved him deeply. So much that I knew she'd forgive any transgressions he'd committed. Seeing her devastation at his near death yesterday had only confirmed it. Even though I'd suspected her claiming Nathan would mean the end of us, I'd encouraged her to do it anyway.

If confronted by the others, I could argue that as a doctor my priority was to save as many lives as possible. Nathan had fatal injuries and Havana bonding with him was his only chance for survival. In only a week, I'd observed her wield incredible power and strength. If anyone could reverse the Alpha male's fate, it was our mate.

But the truth was I'd done it because her happiness meant more than mine. If Nathan died in her arms, she never would have gotten over it. I would do anything to spare her that kind of despair, including setting her free.

A deep ache spread inside my chest. I shoved the Band-Aids inside the overstuffed messenger bag I carried and made my way out of the shop. There was a rack of stuffed polar bears wearing ski jackets near the cash register. On a lark, I grabbed one and crammed it in the bag. Then I exited the shop and headed to the front door.

As I walked around the large wood beam staircase leading to the upper levels, I could hear Nathan and Gabriel arguing.

"Havana told me to check on the survivors." I could hear the scowl in Gabriel's voice.

"And I'm telling you to stay away from them." Nathan's tone was calm but firm. A far cry from the snarling wolf he'd been in the hotel lobby.

Gabriel growled. "I don't take orders from you."

"You will soon," Nathan replied. His confidence was yet another nail in the coffin. "And if you don't want me to compel you to go hike the Himalayas, then you'll keep your distance from the humans. Your death stares are making them uneasy."

Isn't that the truth? I trudged out the door before I could hear Gabriel's response. *Let those wankers pound each other to dust,*

I thought with uncharacteristic darkness. I didn't give a shit. Not when there was little doubt as to what the outcome of this "talk" with Havana would be. *She's going to unclaim me.* I trampled the snow in my path with far more force than necessary.

In the distance, the sun peeked over the snowcapped mountains. I paused, watching the darkness of night succumb to its brilliant glow. Normally, dawn was my favorite time of day bringing with it new possibilities. Not today. Today it brought only disappointment.

As I continued my approach to the hotel, each step seemed heavier than the last. Christ, I didn't want to lose the special connection I had with Havana. She'd reached me in a way no female had before. With a pang of certainty, I knew I'd never find another person, Lykos or human, as special as she was.

All my life I'd had the sense I differed from everyone else and that I was missing something vital. When I found out I'd been adopted, I'd assumed the lost pieces were my biological family. That prompted me to leave my home in Britain and travel to America. I spent months investigating the origins of my birth and when I'd finally transitioned to full Lykos and made my way to Winterhaven, I expected to feel whole. I may not have found my biological mother or father, but at least I'd discovered my true species and finally understood the reasons for my feelings of singularity.

However, that feeling of loss stayed with me. It'd been my constant companion until that fateful night a week ago when Havana claimed me. Then, it vanished, leaving me with an incredible sense of peace and belonging. I mourned losing that and losing her.

I paused on the threshold of the hotel and sucked in a lungful of icy air. *Man up, Mason.* The last thing I wanted was to blubber like a baby when she ended things. Besides, what was that old Tennyson quote? *Better to have loved and lost than to have never loved at all. Right.* I straightened my spine and stepped through the doors.

It took a second for my eyes to adjust to the dim light inside. The sound of a sob drew my gaze toward the reception desk. Havana was leaning against it, sobbing.

All my self-pity went up in smoke. "Don't cry." I rushed to her side.

She looked over at me, her eyes reddened. "Nathan is forcing me to choose between you guys and him."

No surprise there. I nodded slowly. "That's to be expected. Alphas don't share well." *If ever.*

She sank down to the floor and buried her face in her hands. "I-I don't know what to do."

She wants me to help her decide? Bloody hell. I unslung the messenger bag, set it down on top of the desk, and slid down next to her.

Havana scooted closer and rested her head on my shoulder.

I wrapped my arm around her and kissed the top of her head. "It's all going to turn out in the end." It was a phrase one of my teachers at boarding school used to say. Somehow it'd always made me feel better.

She sniffed. "I'm not so sure it will. I don't want to lose you, Gabriel, and Liam."

My heart contracted painfully. "And we don't want to lose you." I knew I could speak for the others in this.

"But Nathan will leave me otherwise and I can't lose him and Mira again." Fresh tears trickled down her cheeks.

I sucked in a pained breath. *It sounds like she's already made her decision.* Since I was expecting it, it shouldn't have felt like a kick to the solar plexus. But it did. Not wanting her to see how hurt I was, I forced a smile. "You know that even if you unclaim us, we'll still be part of your faction... part of your family."

"Really?" She brightened a little.

"Really." The three of us had made an oath to serve her when she'd first transitioned and just because we weren't mated to our Alpha, didn't mean she wasn't still our ruler.

Her smile faded. "I don't think Nathan will go for that."

"He's not in charge now, is he?" I reminded her.

She lifted her head. "No."

"Where we come from, no one tells an Alpha female what to do." I pitied the fool who dared tell Tasha anything she didn't want to hear. Although I didn't want Havana to become a ruthless killer like Tasha, she'd do well to assume some of her self-confidence and strength.

Havana smiled through her tears. "Thank you for the reminder, hon."

"And you don't have to decide right this minute. So dry those beautiful eyes."

"God, I'm sorry. I'm not usually so emotional. I'm not sure what's come over me." She wiped her eyes with the cuff of her robe.

"Don't be hard on yourself." I rubbed her back. "You've been through some traumatic life events in a short while and you've come through it all swimmingly."

She took a deep breath. "It has been a wild ten days, hasn't it?"

"Yes, but we have so much to be thankful for. We have our lives and each other." I squeezed her shoulder. "Oh, and I found a stash of those amazing cheese crackers in the gift shop next door."

"Really? That's awesome news. I'm starving." She rubbed her stomach.

I reached up to grab the messenger bag off the desk. I

must not have zipped it closed because as I was pulling it down, the contents rained down on my head.

Cursing my clumsiness, I gathered up the medical supplies and snack-sized packages of crackers that scattered like confetti around us.

Havana laughed and opened one of the packages that had landed in her lap. "Mmm," she exclaimed biting down on the cracker. She chewed for a second and then made a face.

"What's wrong?"

She frowned. "The taste is off."

"Oh," I inspected the package. "It hasn't expired." I pulled a cracker out and popped it into my mouth. "I don't know what you're talking about. They taste fantastic." I ate two more, enjoying the cheesy crunch. "These will always remind me of that time we sat in the SUV outside the cabin. Do you remember?"

"We polished off a whole box of those crackers," she said with a smile. "You were so sweet to bring me all that stuff."

That reminded me. I looked around and found the stuffed bear lying on its side near her leg. I grabbed it and handed it to her. "Happy Christmas."

Her eyes widened. "It is Christmas morning, isn't it?" She tugged at the bear's stocking cap. "This is cute, hon. Thank you. I always loved Christmas. The decorated tree. The presents..." Her voice trailed off. She looked from the bear to the overturned Christmas tree by the front door. I could see her mind buzzing. When she turned to me, she wore a big smile. "Let's do Christmas for the kids."

I blinked, a bit surprised by her change in mood. "What did you have in mind?"

"Let's clean up the lobby, get that tree back up, and put some presents under it for the Ackerman kids and Mira. Were there any more of these in the shop?" She motioned at the bear. Her excitement was contagious.

I smiled back at her. "They had a whole shelf of them. They also had puzzles and plenty of sweets."

"Mira loves candy!" Havana exclaimed. "This will be fun and after what the kids have been through, they could use some fun."

She had a point although I wasn't sure the other males would agree. Gabriel and Liam didn't strike me as the celebratory types.

Havana rubbed her hands together. "How about I deal with the lobby while you go back to the shop? Bring back anything you think the kids would like."

"Your wish is my command, my lady."

She licked her lips. "God, you sound so sexy when you get all British with me."

"I can get all British inside you too," I said, nibbling her neck.

She pulled away. "I'll take a rain check on that. We'll need all the time we have to get things ready for the kids."

"As long as there is a next time." I tried to keep my tone light, but she had to feel my anxiety.

She looked up at me. "There will definitely be a next time. I-I love you, Mason."

Just hearing her say that unwound the tightness in my chest. "I'm mad for you." I leaned down and pressed my mouth against hers. I meant it to be a quick peck on the lips, but she opened her mouth in an invitation I couldn't ignore. The kiss instantly turned erotic.

As our tongues danced, my hands somehow found their way inside her robe. I palmed the soft weight of her breasts, and then slid my hand between her legs.

She parted them for me and moaned when I rubbed her clitoris in little circles. "Oh, yes!"

I don't know exactly how it happened, but one second we were upright, the next she was sprawled out on the floor underneath me. Her robe fell open and every inch of her honey-colored skin pressed against me. "I've changed my mind," she gasped, "fuck me, Mason."

"Are you sure?" I asked, my erection attempting to punch a hole through my borrowed slacks.

She wrapped her bare legs around my hips. "We have to be quick."

Quick? But this may be the last time we're together. I stilled at the painful thought. I wanted to take my time and brand the experience into my mind forever, but she had other ideas.

She quickly freed me and aligned our bodies.

One rub of her wet center and I was a goner. Instinct took over and with one thrust I was home—gloved inside her scorching wet heat. *Bloody hell*, she felt amazing.

"Faster," she begged, pushing up off the carpet.

Giving her what she needed, I rode her harder than I ever had before.

She loved it, bucking senselessly underneath me. With a muffled scream against the collar of my shirt, she came.

My orgasm blasted through me like an avalanche. I threw back my head and surged into her one final time. Then falling down on my forearms, I kissed her panting lips and savored the incredible feeling of connection and belonging. For that brief moment in time, I pretended it would last forever.

18

HAVANA

My body hummed with a sexual afterglow as I tidied up the lobby. Trying hard not to think about the decision I'd soon be forced to make, I added another log to the fire and checked in on my mates. *"How's it going, Mason?"*

"Good. I found some child-size ski jackets and some coloring books to add to the gift pile. I'll bring them over shortly."

"Perfect! Pick up some for Isaac and Lily too." We were setting aside gifts for the older kids so when we got back to Sanctuary, they could have their own Christmas.

Switching mental channels, I asked Liam the same question I'd been asking for the past two hours. *"Are the kids up yet?"*

The gentle giant chuckled into my mind. *"Not yet, beautiful. I promise to alert you the moment they wake."*

"Thank you." I paused for a second. *"Are Nathan and Gabriel still going at it?"*

"Yeah. They're just arguing though. No fists." He sounded disappointed.

I shook my head. *"I can't believe it. They're grown ass men acting like—"*

Liam interrupted me. *"They're Lykos, not men. This is normal for the male members of our species."*

"It is?" Damn, I had a lot to learn.

"I take that back. It's normal for Beta males to fight for dominance over each other. Normally, no one challenges an Alpha male except for another Alpha male, but Gabriel always was different. He never backs down from a fight. Tasha used to say he was Alpha in every way but his eyes. I think that's why she made him Head Enforcer."

"Ugh, that's probably why she stuck that yellow diamond in his eye." My stomach churned at the thought of Gabriel suffering for so long.

"Probably, she's pretty twisted like that."

After seeing some of Nathan's memories, twisted didn't even come close to covering it. Tasha was a maniacal bitch. I planned on using my power to rid the world of her crazy ass, but first things first. *"Remember to let me know the minute the kids wake."*

"Will do." He hesitated for a moment. *"Do you think we might have some alone time later?"*

Anxiety and a hint of sexual frustration wove through our bond.

"Of course." My breath sped up as I imagined a sexy romp with him after the festivities. Further corrupting the former virgin was high on my list of favorite activities. *"What did you have in mind?"*

"Us, in the pool," he quickly responded.

"That sounds amazing." Heat moved low in my body and my clit throbbed. Despite all the sex I'd had today, I craved more. Transitioning into a Lykos had turned me into a full-blown nympho, but at least I had plenty of mates to satisfy my appetite. *For now,* my inner voice reminded me.

My stomach tightened. I knew Nathan would force me to make a choice soon, but I didn't want to focus on that now. Mason was right. I didn't have to decide this minute. It was Christmas, a day for celebrating. *I'll rock your world in the pool later on today, big guy, but first—*

"I'll tell you when the kids wake up," he finished for me.

Laughing, I ended our mental conversation. For half a second, I considered checking in with Nathan and Gabriel, but quickly dismissed the idea. Their behavior was pissing me off. "Why can't we all just get along?" I said to the side table filled with snacks and drinks I'd raided from the vending machines down the hall. I could've found better food upstairs in the restaurant, but we'd piled the dead bodies out on the restaurant balcony, and my sour tummy couldn't handle the stink. *This will have to do. At least we have a Christmas tree.*

With a critical eye, I swept my gaze over the now upright Christmas tree. Although there was no electricity to illuminate the strings of lights, the flames from the fireplace made the colorful glass bulbs shimmer and the tinsel glisten. The majestic tree could've starred in one of those TV Christmas specials I used to watch as a child. Especially with the mountains of presents stacked underneath it.

While tidying up the lobby, I'd found dozens of suitcases and bags behind the front desk. Hoping the dead didn't mind me poaching, I'd gone through them and found quite a few wrapped packages. Even though I had no clue what the gifts were, I threw them under the tree too. The metallic sheen of the wrapping paper added a nice touch.

I bent down to move one gift closer to the tree. My stomach lurched violently. I held my breath waiting for the feeling of nausea to pass. *Damn. Did I catch some kind of werewolf flu or something?* Puking all over the presents was a sure-fire way to ruin the celebration.

Remembering a container of antacid among all the crap in

Mason's messenger bag, I headed over to the front desk and pulled the bag open.

Aha! There it was under a bottle of Tylenol. As I pulled the container out, a white box with pink lettering caught my eye. "One step pregnancy test," I read aloud. *Seriously, why the hell would Mason grab that? And why the hell would a ski resort shop even sell that in the first place?* I chuckled until my stomach shifted again.

Damn. This is getting old. Maybe I need to eat something. I eyed a package of crackers. My stomach churned. *Nope.*

The white box drew my eye again. *No way. You don't think...* I shook my head in denial, but my fingers curled around the box as if on their own accord.

What would it hurt to test? With shaking hands I carried the box to the closest bathroom. It was pitch-black inside, but I had no trouble seeing. *Go werewolf night vision!* I found a stall, opened the box and pulled out the plastic stick. From living through several of my friend's pregnancy scares over the years, I knew the drill.

After peeing on the absorbent strip, I put the cap on the stick, and went over to the sink to wash my hands. *No water. Right. Damn.* I grabbed the test and brought it back out to the lobby. I set it next to Mason's bag and dug out one of the bottles of hand sanitizer he'd stuck in the front pocket. As I rubbed the aloe-scented gel between my palms, I looked over at the indicator.

Two bright pink lines stared back at me.

Oh. My. God. My heart skipped a beat. Even though I knew damn well what those lines meant, I ran back into the bathroom, grabbed the box, and compared the indicator with the example picture. There was no mistake.

The world started to spin.

I'm pregnant...

A million thoughts bombarded me. *How could this happen*

with an IUD? How am I going to take care of a baby? A freaking werewolf baby. Whose baby is it? Gabriel's? Liam's? Mason's? How will Nathan react? Oh, God what if there's a whole litter of babies in there?

I started hyperventilating.

Four male voices immediately crashed into my mind.

"Vana, what's wrong?"

"Havana, are you okay?"

"Are you under attack?"

"I'll be right there, love!"

I took a steadying breath and brought the chaos of my emotions under control. I sure as hell didn't want my mates losing their shit over this and ruining the celebration. Making sure my thoughts were locked down tight, I said, *"I'm fine, everyone. I just saw a rat. The lobby is ready, Liam, are the kids—"*

"Still sleeping, but I'll wake them now."

"No! Don't wake them," I said quickly.

The sound of the front door opening had me spinning around.

Mason ran into the lobby. "Where's the rat? I'll take care of it."

"Thank you, my mighty warrior." I quickly stuffed the white box and pregnancy test back into the messenger bag before he could see it. I needed time to process this before I shared the news with anyone. "The vile thing scurried off toward the elevators." I motioned down the hall. "But don't worry about the rat. Get those gifts under the tree."

"Yes, madam," he said, bowing.

Realizing I was being shrewish, I apologized. "This means a lot to me, Mason. As a kid, I spent most of my holidays alone—my mom was always working or with one of her boyfriends. I'd watch Christmas specials on television and see other families celebrating together. I dreamed one day I'd have that..." I cleared my throat. "But this isn't about me."

Mostly. "This is about giving a little hope and cheer to kids who've just gone through hell."

Mason reached out and took my hand. "It's a noble sentiment." He squeezed my hand before dropping it.

While he arranged the new gifts under the tree, I turned the armchairs so they faced the door.

Now everything is ready.

Liam's voice boomed in my mind. *"Everyone is up. We're headed your way."*

"Perfect timing!" My stomach swirled with excitement.

Finished with his task, Mason walked over to me. "It looks very festive." He wrapped his arm around my shoulder. "You know, you'll never be alone for another holiday. Not while I draw breath."

"Thank you, hon." *He's right.* I would never be alone again. Instinctively, I curved my hands over my stomach. I was pregnant. *Holy crap.* The emotions I'd been trying to keep at bay swamped me. Confusion, excitement, and a love so intense it rattled my bones. Even though this pregnancy couldn't have happened at a worse time, and it meant shifting my priorities and plans, I already adored my child.

I'll do whatever it takes to be a good mom. Unlike my mother, I'd put my child's needs before my own and I'd make damn sure they knew who their father was.

Next to me, Mason stiffened. His all too perceptive gaze focused on the placement of my hands. I could see the questions swirling in his deep blue eyes.

Crap. I was no good at keeping secrets.

"Love, are you—"

The sound of chattering voices interrupted him. People streamed into the hotel.

With a surge of satisfaction, I saw the tense expressions of the survivors soften as they looked around the decorated lobby.

Gabriel stalked in looking more annoyed than angry, which was probably as much as I could hope for. After nodding at Mason, the dark-haired warrior took position on my right side. "I don't see the point of all this," he grumbled. "It's delaying us from returning to Sanctuary."

"Chill and be happy for a minute. That's an order." I softened my command with a wink.

"About time someone forces that male to relax," Liam said, walking over to us. He held baby Sierra cradled in his arms. The nine-month-old had a clump of his chest hair in her chubby fist, but Liam didn't seem to mind. He shifted her to the side so he could kiss me.

My gentle giant will make a wonderful father. They all will. I looked from Liam to Gabriel who had wrapped a protective arm around me. I knew without a doubt that Gabriel would let nothing harm our children, even if that meant giving his own life to protect them. I looked over at Mason who'd shifted slightly away to let Gabriel hold me. The gorgeous blond doctor would be such a patient and loving dad. And Nathan had already proven to be an amazing father—

"Vana!" Mira cried, racing through the door. She bypassed the Christmas tree, stepped around Liam, and launched herself at me.

Pulling away from Gabriel, I caught her.

The little girl threw her arms around my neck. "I thought you'd left again. I don't ever want you to leave. Promise you won't leave."

"I promise I won't leave, love bug." I kissed the top of her tangled silver-streaked hair. Mira needed a bath and some hair combing. Making a mental note to clean her and the other children after the festivities, I said, "Now why don't you check out those presents under the tree before the boys open everything." I knelt to set her down and watched her join the Ackerman children in digging through the piles of gifts.

Many of the adult survivors had made their way over to the table of food. Although most wore guarded expressions, and spoke in hushed voices, they did eat a little. Those poor people. I could only imagine what they'd lived through. I'd look after them from now on and as soon as they were safe at Sanctuary, I'd head to Sunridge and search for more survivors there. Then I'd do the same for every town from here to Saguaro Valley.

A large shadow fell over me. I looked up and met Nathan's golden gaze.

"Does your promise to Mira mean what I think it does?" He gave Gabriel a smug look.

"Yes and no." I'd realized that Nathan couldn't force me to choose. As much as I loved him, I also cared deeply for the others and at least one of them had fathered my child. I would never separate my child from their dad. Not after growing up fatherless myself.

Nathan would be pissed to learn he had to share me, but he'd eventually get over it. *I hope.* He could very well make good on his threat to leave me, but based on what I knew of the mating bonds, it would be impossible for him to go far. He was mine, and I refused to let him go. *I'm the Alpha female, damn it. It's time I act like it.* Filled with resolve, I pushed myself to standing. I must've move too fast because the lobby swirled around me. Stumbling, I fell forward.

Four sets of muscular arms reached to steady me.

"Little wolf, what's wrong?"

"You look pale, beautiful."

"Princess, are you ill?"

"You've been overdoing it, love."

"I'm fine." I brushed my mates' hands away only to be hit with another wave of vertigo. *Damn.* I needed to eat something even if my stomach said otherwise.

Mason threaded his arm through mine. "You should sit down."

"Good idea." Nathan grabbed my other arm.

Gabriel looked over at the fireplace. "Bring her to one of the chairs. I'll make the humans move."

"I'll help," Liam called out.

The two warriors stalked ahead of us. One look at their faces and the poor survivors scattered like fish in the path of sharks.

I fought to hide my smile as my mates settled me in the closest armchair. I'd made my decision all right. How fortunate that my baby and I had four princes instead of one. *And we'll have our happy-ever-after.* I gently laid my hand on my abdomen. *Oh yes, we will.*

DID YOU ENJOY THIS BOOK?

I'd be so appreciative if you left a review on Amazon or any other reader site or blog you frequent. I prioritize continuing series based on the reviews I receive so if you would like to see more of Havana and her mates let me know!

The adventure continues with Book Three.

CLAIMING HER MATES: BOOK THREE

For us to live, the bitch must die...

The happy-ever-after I'm seeking seems farther away than ever. Nathan refuses to accept my other mates and the secret I'm keeping may destroy any possible future between the five of us.

Even worse, Tasha's arrival puts us all in grave danger. No one takes what is hers and lives.

Our only chance for survival is to defeat the psychotic Alpha female. But how can we kill an immortal?

ABOUT THE AUTHOR

Dia wanted to be a writer from the time she could hold a pencil. A lover of paranormal romance, reverse harem, science fiction, urban fantasy, and horror, she writes action-packed stories featuring kick-butt heroines and the alpha male heroes who fall for them.

If you want to be notified when the next book in the series releases please sign up for my newsletter on my website.

https://diacole.com/

BOOKS BY DIA COLE

Heaven Before Hell

Lover in Hell

Heaven in Hell: Boxed Set (Episodes 1-4)

Heaven in Hell: Boxed Set (Episodes 5—8)

Undead Worlds 2 Anthology (Breakfast in Hell)

Claiming The Nanny (Claiming Her Mates prequel)

Claiming Her Mates: Book One

Claiming Her Mates: Book Two

Claiming Her Mates: Book Three

Claiming the Bride

Reforming the Witch

Claiming the Witch

Claiming the Moon Hunter

EXCERPT FROM CLAIMING HER MATES: BOOK THREE

❦   I   ❧

HAVANA

C*hristmas Day...*

THE DECORATIONS ON THE SKI RESORT CHRISTMAS TREE shook as three children gleefully tore through colorfully wrapped gifts beneath its boughs. Their laughter filled me with joy.

Sinking into the warm embrace of my armchair, I inhaled the wintery aroma of the garland strung around picture windows overlooking silvery banks of snow. The fragrance mixed wonderfully with the smoky scent of the fire crackling in the rustic fireplace.

It all was so damn near perfect I could almost ignore the bloodstains on the carpet, the lingering odor of rot in the air, and the gnawing feeling that something terrible was going to happen.

Taking a deep breath, I tried to stomp out the irrational anxiety. We'd all survived our hellish encounters with the dead yesterday and I wasn't going to let anything ruin the celebration. I'd been dreaming about having a real Christmas with decorations, presents, and a family my entire life. The closest I'd ever come to it as a lonely child had been the television specials I'd watched from my mom's dirty trailer floor. This was so much better than a scripted show.

Over by the Christmas tree, the Ackerman boys and Mira, the daughter of my newest mate, let out ecstatic cries as they tore through the wrapped gifts like pint-sized tornados.

I couldn't help but laugh at their excitement.

I wasn't alone. Several of the human survivors milling around the snack table cracked a smile too. Seeing the terror and shock slowly leave their eyes warmed my heart. Those poor people had been through so much watching their friends and family members die. *They don't need to be frightened any longer.* I sat up straighter in my chair. With my new abilities, I could protect them from the dead.

But can I protect them from what's coming? Doubt heightened my feeling of unease.

Trying to shake off the premonition, I focused instead on the gorgeous, muscular males surrounding my armchair. All four of my mates were anxious over my dizzy spell a few moments ago, but they didn't need to worry. There was a good reason for my vertigo. I gently laid my palm over my abdomen trying to sense the spark of new life growing inside me.

We're going to have a baby! My chest tightened with happiness and excitement. All my life I'd wanted to have a big family. I just never figured on my children having so many daddies. I bit my lower lip to muffle my giggle. Soon, I'd have to spill my secret to my mates, but not now. Now I just wanted to enjoy our first holiday together.

A soft sound drew my attention to Liam, my seven-foot-tall auburn haired teddy bear of a mate who sat in the armchair across from mine. The nine-month-old infant he cradled against his bare chest sucked on his right knuckle as he hummed her a lullaby.

"You're great with Sierra," I said with a smile. *He'll be an awesome father.*

Liam stroked his hand through the baby's silky tuff of dark hair. "She's a pretty babe, isn't she?"

I nodded. "She's precious. I'm so glad she's okay."

"Me too." Liam met my gaze and we shared the horrible memory of the helicopter crash yesterday. It was a miracle everyone survived.

A loud shriek drew my attention back to the tree. Sierra's oldest brother, Kaden, was holding a stuffed bear over the head of three-year-old Jackson.

Mira tried to grab the bear from Kaden. "Give it back to him."

Kaden shook his head. "He's trying to eat the hat."

Despite the older boy being considerably taller than her, Mira put her hands on her hips and stared into his eyes. "Give Jackson his bear!" Even from over here, I heard the otherworldly ring in her tone.

Kaden's expression went slack and he immediately dropped the stuffed toy into his brother's outreached hands.

Ah, hell. Mira was using compulsion. Again.

"Good." Mira threw back her silver-streaked hair. "And give me your candy cane."

Without so much as blinking, the older boy reached for his candy.

Shaking my head, I looked over at Nathan to see if he was watching his daughter break the rules.

The Alpha male stood nose to nose with Gabriel, my most aggressive mate, oblivious to anything but their telepathic argument.

Seeing that he'd be no help, I mentally chided Mira. *"Stop compelling Kaden this instant."*

The headstrong little girl jerked her head in my direction, a surprised look on her face. *"You're talking to me like Daddy does."*

I didn't know that Nathan spoke with her telepathically. I wondered what else the little girl knew of our species. *"Should we tell him you're using compulsion?"* I pretended to look for Nathan behind my chair.

Her eyes rounded and she shook her head. *"I'm sorry. I'll stop."*

"Why don't you unwrap more presents?" I suggested.

"Okay." She grabbed the closest gift, tore off the wrapping paper, and held up a bottle of champagne. "Look, Vana! I got some juice."

I coughed. "That's great, love bug." Maybe tossing in the random gifts I'd found in the luggage behind the front desk hadn't been the best idea. *God only knows what else the kids might find.*

The handsome blond doctor sitting in the armchair next to mine called out, "Let me see that juice, Miss Mira. It may have medicinal properties." He stood and wiped away an imaginary wrinkle on his slacks. Only Mason would manage to scrounge up a pair of clean pants and a collared shirt. While he looked as dignified as ever, the rest of us looked like half-dressed hobos.

Mira glared at Mason. "No. It's mine." She clutched the bottle tightly to her chest and pouted like only a four-year-old could.

"Bollocks. That's a 1959 Dom Perignon." Mason's telepathic voice carried his sexy British accent.

I laughed. *"Don't worry. She'll forget about it if you offer her that."* I nodded in the direction of a royal blue velvet box I'd set on a side table. The box contained an antique diamond butterfly hairpin I knew Mira would love.

"What if she refuses?"

"She won't." No female of any age could resist diamonds that size. As if on their own accord, my fingers slid into the front pocket of the white terry-cloth robe I wore. The stunning engagement ring Nathan gave me a few hours ago was still there. I absently rubbed the four-carat princess cut diamond still shocked at discovering Nathan had planned on proposing to me instead of breaking up with me that terrible night all those months ago.

I wished I could take back the river of tears I'd cried over him since that night. Even though I now knew the truth—he'd broken up with me to save me from his ex—the memory of the pain he'd put me through still stung.

Mason kissed my cheek. *"All right, here goes nothing."* He strode over to the table, picked up the velvet box, and then walked over to Mira.

The little girl turned and smiled at the doctor. Her amber eyes, so like Nathan's, brightened.

I twisted my head around, hoping her father was watching the exchange.

Nathan and Gabriel growled at each other. Evenly matched in their six-foot-four height, they both possessed the muscular build of NFL linemen and they both were barely dressed. I hummed my approval as the flannel blanket knotted around Nathan's waist dipped low enough to show the taut muscles of his six-pack.

I licked my lips hoping the blanket might slip further. From our steamy encounter in this very chair, I knew Nathan wore nothing under it. My skin warmed and my nipples hardened in memory of our makeup sex. I could definitely go for more of that right now.

"You're mistaken, Ambassador. Havana is mated to us all."

Gabriel flexed one of his huge biceps drawing my gaze to his gorgeous bronze skin. The dark-haired male wore only a pair of jeans so tattered I could clearly see his muscular thighs. My breathing quickened as I remembered Gabriel using those powerful muscles to pound into me at the resort pool just a little while ago.

"Not for long." Nathan chuckled. "I've asked Vana to choose between us. Who do you think she'll pick? Three males that were strangers two weeks ago or the male whose engagement ring she carries in her pocket?"

And just like that my bubble of happiness popped and a pit formed in my stomach.

Nathan continued. "You'll understand if I don't invite you to our wedding, Enforcer."

Gabriel snarled.

Crap. I clenched Nathan's engagement ring so tightly it dug into the palm of my hand. *Why can't he accept my other mates?* There had to be some way of convincing Nathan to give the five of us a chance. *We can work. I know it.*

Liam looked over at me. *"Ignore them, Beautiful. Focus on the kids. They're having a good time, aren't they?"*

He's right. I won't let Nathan and Gabriel ruin this. I dropped the engagement ring back into my pocket and looked over at Mira.

The little girl danced around the tree clutching her new butterfly hairpin.

Mason raised the bottle of champagne in my direction. *"It worked."*

I started to congratulate him, but soft footsteps stole my attention.

Rebecca, a middle-aged woman with greying hair and deep laugh lines around her mouth, approached. "I can take my granddaughter now." She held her arms outstretched to Liam. To her credit her hands only shook slightly. I gave the older woman props. Few would try to take anything from a male Liam's size. My respect for the woman, who'd apparently been the principal of an elementary school, grew.

Liam hesitated for a split second and then gently transitioned the sleeping baby to Rebecca.

Cradling Sierra against her chest with practiced ease, Rebecca turned her attention to me. "Are we moving to another location?"

I nodded. "We're going to caravan up the mountain to Sanctuary. The lodge there has enough supplies for everyone." There was no safer place for us all to ride out the apocalypse. Sanctuary had running water and electricity along with enough food and supplies to last us for years. Thank God, Nathan had ordered Liam, Mason, and Gabriel to bring me there ten days ago. If they hadn't... I shivered imagining what might have happened.

Rebecca gazed at the tightly clustered group of survivors. "Marshall has convinced some of the others that we should stay."

I glanced at the thin, balding man gesturing wildly to the others. Marshall had been someone important—a company vice president, CEO, or some crap like that. It didn't matter. He along with everyone else would need to stick with my crew if they wanted to survive.

Liam stood, the top of his head nearly scraping the slanted wood beam ceiling. "Tell Marshall, he does what Havana says or he'll die."

Rebecca took a step back.

Although my mate needed to work on his delivery, I appreciated him having my back. "What Liam means is that it will be safer for everyone at Sanctuary." At some point, any zombies in the nearby town would head here in search for living prey. *Is that the threat I sense?*

Rebecca nodded. "I'll talk to them." She marched over to

the group of survivors. Within minutes the humans were arguing.

Humans. Crap. Listen to me. When did I start thinking that way?

Over by the tree, Mira was trying to yank the champagne bottle out of Mason's hands. "Give me my juice."

"Miss Mira, we made a trade fair and square. Your juice for the diamond heirloom."

The little girl stamped her foot. "No!"

Mason sent me a helpless look.

Time for her dad to get involved. I turned my head. "Nathan can you..."

Mira's father shoved Gabriel. "I'll pound you into dust, Enforcer."

Gabriel bared his teeth and pushed Nathan back. "Do you really want another ass kicking, Ambassador?"

Both of the males' hair stood on end and their eyes sparked with aggression.

Goddamn it. They were going to fight. Again.

As my annoyance rose, I pinched the bridge of my nose wondering if I should make good on my threat to compel the two to be friends.

"Let's take this outside," growled Nathan.

Irritation morphed into worry as I watched the two males stalk outside. *I have to stop them.*

As I pushed myself to my feet, Liam dragged me into his lap. "Let them work it out."

"Nathan might not survive another encounter." The Alpha male had been pretty messed up from his fight with Gabriel just a few hours earlier and that was on top of him nearly dying yesterday.

Liam snorted. "Don't worry. Gabriel knows Nathan is mated to you and if one of your mates dies, we all die. He won't risk your life."

Liam's words eased some of my anxiety.

"But they're ruining Christmas." I hated that my eyes filled with tears. *Damn hormones.* "All I wanted was for all of us to have a real freaking holiday experience." *Is that too much to ask?*

"This is the real holiday experience." Liam gave me a wry grin. "At least all of mine were like this. Children screaming. Males fighting."

"Really?"

He chuckled. "Usually my mom threw me and my brothers outside before we could destroy her furniture."

I blinked trying to picture a family of giants. "Were all your brothers as large as you?"

"No." His smile faded. "My mother always said I was a freak of nature." His shame and embarrassment leaked through our bond.

How could any mother say that to their child, much less to Liam? He was the sweetest guy ever. I wrapped my arms around his waist and hugged him. "You're not a freak, you're perfect and I'm so glad you're mine."

Liam gave me a swoon worthy smile and whispered in my ear, "Do you think we could have that alone time now?" He telepathically replayed our earlier conversation where I'd promised him some one-on-one time in the pool.

"Right now?" I glanced out the window seeing nothing but fluffy white snow. Gabriel and Nathan must have taken their fight away from the resort.

Across the room, Mason pleaded with Mira while the Ackerman boys ran in circles around them shrieking loudly.

The racket had woken Sierra who screeched like a dying peacock.

Rebecca tried to shush the baby back to sleep while Marshall shouted, "It's suicide to leave. We have everything we need."

"But Nathan said we should go to Sanctuary," another survivor cried.

Marshall narrowed his watery eyes. "Screw Nathan."

"Nathan should have let the zombies eat that guy," Liam muttered. "Come on, let's get out of here."

I sighed and rubbed my temples. This definitely was not the Christmas of my dreams. "As tempting as your offer is, I need to fix this." *First I'll deal with Gabriel and Nathan and then I'll set the humans straight.*

Liam cupped my face in his hands. "This will all be here in an hour. Escape with me for a little while. Let me worship you."

"Worship?"

He nodded eagerly. "From the top of your head to your beautiful toes."

Heat curled between my thighs. That sounded pretty amazing. I looked over the chaotic lobby. *I'll bet no one will notice if we skip out for a bit.* "Lead the way, big guy."

He grinned from ear to ear and dragged me down the hallway.

2

HAVANA

Despite his large size, Liam walked softly and not a single person turned their head when we ducked down the hallway and pushed through a door near the elevators.

We stopped inside the pitch-black room.

The bleachy smell of chlorine and the lingering scent of the passion I'd shared with Gabriel filled the air. The erotic memories of my time with the dark-haired male made my nipples pebble against the terry cloth fabric of my robe.

Liam whirled around, hauled me into his arms, and kissed me. He tasted of candy canes and chocolate, an intoxicating flavor I couldn't get enough of.

Kicking off my flip-flops, I wrapped my legs around his waist and pressed myself flush against him.

Our lips and tongues slow danced and then, as if some inaudible song had quickened its beat, our kiss deepened. Desire, hot and sweet, drugged my mind.

He kneaded my ass, while I caressed his broad shoulders and ripped biceps. His body was a thing of beauty and I wanted to savor every inch especially the impressive bulge pressing insistently against the fly of his jeans.

Moaning, I sucked his tongue into my mouth and rocked my hips against him.

"Havana," Liam panted. He tried to slip his hand under my robe, but I'd belted it tightly. He cursed under his breath and tugged the fabric apart.

The light tinkling sound of metal hitting the pool deck made me break our kiss and look down.

Nathan's engagement ring lay next to Liam's right foot.

Crap. It must have fallen out of my pocket.

Liam tensed, his expression falling. "So Nathan was telling the truth. He asked you to marry him?"

I sighed. "He did."

"Will you?"

I paused, not having really considered it until now. The five of us were already soul bonded, did we really need the pomp and circumstance of a wedding? But then again, the idea of a romantic ceremony where we cemented our love for each other had a lot of appeal. "I'd like to marry him at the same time I marry you, Mason, and Gabriel." What a wedding that would be. Syd, my best friend, and I had fanta-sized about our weddings together. She'd flip her lid if she knew mine would involve more than one groom. *Ah, hell.* I hoped she was safe somewhere.

Liam let out a deep breath. "You'd marry me?" Our bond thrummed with his relief and happiness.

"Hell, yes." I rose on the balls of my feet to kiss him.

He stared down at my lips. "But Nathan won't go for that. He wants you to choose."

"Fuck choosing." I grabbed the back of his head and forced his lips to meet mine. I wasn't giving up any of my mates.

The kiss quickly turned toe-curling hot. I thought for sure

he'd rip off my robe and take me against the door. Instead, he pulled away and scanned the room. "Jacuzzi or the pool?" His werewolf vision, like mine, allowed him to see both the lap-pool and the Jacuzzi perfectly in the dark.

Although both options were fine, I felt drawn to the hot tub. "How about the Jacuzzi?" The water would be cold and the jets wouldn't work without electricity, but we could sit down in there—or rather, I could sit on Liam in there. My heart pounded while my dirty mind raced with possibilities. The tub was even big enough to accommodate all my mates if they joined us.

All my mates...

The idea of all four males in the water... kissing me... touching me.... loving me... made heat move low in my body. *Of course, Nathan and Gabriel have to stop punching each other long enough to pay attention to me. Bastards.*

"Jacuzzi it is." Liam tugged me through the maze of lounge chairs and tables until we got to the hot tub. Then he stopped at the edge and dipped his bare foot into the water. He frowned. "The water is cold."

"I'm sure we could heat it up," I said, winking.

Lust sparked through our connection. He turned toward me and reached for the belt of my robe.

Not so fast. Despite having sex multiple times, Liam and I had never been together alone. The other guys had always been there. I wanted this time to be special for my former virgin. I brushed his hands away and smiled coyly. "Sit down for a minute." I gestured at the nearby lounge chair.

His brows knit together. "You don't want me to take off your robe?"

"No." Before his expression could fall, I added, "I want to take it off for you." I didn't have many marketable skills, but I sure as hell knew how to undress in front of a guy. "Sit down and I'll give you a show."

Liam's eyes widened and he licked his lips. "Okay." Never taking his eyes from me, he dropped back onto the lounge chair.

With a loud snapping sound, the vinyl straps broke and Liam fell straight through to the floor.

Oh, no! "Liam! Are you okay?"

He sat up, his face reddening. "Yeah, guess these things aren't meant for males my size."

I felt terrible as he pushed himself out of the destroyed chair and shoved it across the pool deck. "I'm sorry. I didn't think—"

"Don't apologize," he said interrupting me. "That kind of thing has been happening all my life. Freak of nature, remember?"

My heart tripped over itself. I couldn't believe this gorgeous, magnificent male thought so poorly of himself. If I ever met his mother, I'd kick her in the crotch. "You're no freak of nature and I never want to hear you say that again." I needed to show him how much I appreciated him, supersize and all.

"Yes, my Alpha," he said, with a much more genuine smile.

I tossed my hair back. "I've changed my mind about the chair. You stand right there."

He froze as if I'd compelled him not to move.

"Relax, big guy. We're going to have some fun." I circled my mate, admiring his incredibly broad chest. I traced my hands across it, loving the soft springy auburn chest hair so different from my other mates. "You have bigger guns than anyone I've ever seen." I caressed his shredded biceps, thinking of the body builder I'd dated years ago. That guy had won the Southwest Body Building Championship and his body didn't hold a candle to Liam's ripped physique.

Liam growled softly under his breath. "I'll kill him whoever he is."

I laughed realizing he must've been picking up on my thoughts. "That guy's a loser and I haven't seen him in years." Given the state of the world these days, I'd likely never see him again. "Besides, he didn't have muscles like this." I ran my hand down his stomach, loving the way his rock hard abs danced.

Liam sucked in a breath as I unbuttoned his fly and released his massive cock.

An erotic thrill shot through me as it swelled and throbbed in my hands. His shaft was a thing of beauty, as long as my forearm and as thick as his wrists. I couldn't even wrap my fingers fully around it. I wet my lips thinking of how no male had ever filled me the way Liam had. A hungry ache stirred between my thighs.

A strange half growl-half purring sound filled the air.

Liam's gaze flew to my lips and I realized the noise was coming from me.

Getting a grip on my lust before I tackled him to the floor, I stepped away. "Take off your pants."

Liam quickly kicked off his jeans, the fabric landing on the pieces of the broken chair.

"Now go wait for me in the Jacuzzi."

My mate quickly stepped into the tub and obediently sat down. The cold seemed to have no effect on his cock as the smooth, pink crown breached the surface of the water. "What else do you want, my Alpha?"

Good question. I smiled. Although I enjoyed being dominated during sex, being in control came naturally to me. *Hell.* I'd played a dominatrix on stage for years. After being so thoroughly worked over by Gabriel earlier, I needed to feel more in control of my body. Also, I sensed Liam would enjoy a little power play. "Now I want you to watch."

I slowly undid my belt, keeping my robe from gaping open. Then, I danced seductively for him revealing an inch of my skin at a time.

Liam's breathing grew labored—our bond simmering with lust.

Wanting to rock his world, I threw off the robe and cupped my breasts in my hands.

He inhaled sharply when I pinched my nipples.

"Do you enjoy watching me?" I slid one leg up on the Jacuzzi handrail. The position exposed my sex to his hungry gaze.

"Fuck yeah," he gasped, rising out of the water. Impossibly his massive cock had grown even larger.

"I'll touch mine if you touch yours." I caressed the hard points of my nipples, loving the way his pupils dilated. Then I slid my hand between my legs, careful to keep my balance.

Liam groaned and wrapped his fist around himself.

"That's it. I want to see you touch yourself." I rubbed teasing circles around my clit.

He moaned my name and ran his fist from crown to root.

"Faster," I ordered, loving the way he bit down on his lower lip.

He complied, thrusting his hips in time to the rhythm of his hand.

Watching him pleasure himself cranked my desire even higher. My core ached with wanting, growing wetter and wetter. "I can't wait until I have you inside me."

His hand moved so fast over his hard flesh it was a blur.

"That's it, baby. I'm going to fuck you so hard, just like this." I inserted two fingers inside my wet channel and rocked against them.

He made a choking sound, his pupils dilating to the point his eyes were nearly all black.

Then moving impossibly fast for a man his size, he

reached up and dragged me off the rail. Using enviable strength, he held me by my hips just over the icy water. My core was pressed right against the tip of his engorged cock.

God, this is going to feel so good. I had two seconds to savor the feeling of his throbbing erection poised right where I needed it. Then, with one punch of his hips, he was sliding inside me, claiming me...

DID YOU ENJOY THIS PREVIEW?

You can find the book here: https://
mybook.to/ClaimingHerMates2

Please don't forget to leave a review if you enjoyed this work!

Thank you for reading!

www.ingramcontent.com/pod-product-compliance
Lightning Source LLC
Chambersburg PA
CBHW050531190726

48284CB00003B/1022